The
Ironside
Heist

A Pierce Spruce
Adventure Novel

The Ironside Heist: A Pierce Spruce Adventure Novel by David Lowe Cozad

Copyright © 2022 David Lowe Cozad

Cover and Interior design by Jacqueline Cook

ISBN: 978-1-7366203-6-6 (Paperback)
ISBN: 978-1-7366203-7-3 (e-book)

10 9 8 7 6 5 4 3 2 1

BISAC Subject Headings:
FIC002000 FICTION / Action & Adventure
FIC050000 / FICTION / Crime
FIC022100 / FICTION / Mystery & Detective / Amateur Sleuth
FIC030000 / FICTION / Thrillers / Suspense

Address all correspondence to:
Fireship Press, LLC
P.O. Box 68412
Tucson, AZ 85737

Visit our website at:
www.fireshippress.com

For Harry Benjamin Lowe.
A man who loved a good adventure.

The Ironside Heist

A Pierce Spruce
Adventure Novel

David Lowe Cozad

Cortero Publishing
An Imprint of FIRESHIP PRESS

Prologue

"Mr. Director, you wanted to see me?"

"Thank you for coming to my office, Special Agent Graham. There's something I need to run by you regarding your investigation of *The Response*."

"Do we have more information?"

"You're aware at this point about the disappearance of the statue in Boston, the one of *Colonel William Prescott*?"

"Yes, sir, I just found out about it from the analysts about 20 minutes ago. Does this mean I'm on the next flight to Logan?"

"Not quite. I want you to stick around with the analysts to try and gather some more intelligence. The heists have been occurring in bundles lately. I expect *The Response* has a few more in mind before they leave Boston. The USS *Constitution* could be one of them."

"Boston later this week, then?"

"London will be your next stop."

"*The Response* isn't in London, sir. Unless Archie Neville went there without us knowing."

"Neville is still in Vermont. You're going to London because I'm thinking about bringing a friend of mine in on the operation."

"I thought the president said no one else could be brought in on this. Something about not wanting to use any more government resources?"

"You let me worry about the president. Plus, my friend isn't on the government's payroll."

"Okay, Mr. Director. But can you at least give me a name of who I will be meeting in London?"

"Pierce Spruce."

"The billionaire?"

"Yes. Pierce Spruce the billionaire."

"Why would a billionaire from London come to Boston to help the FBI?"

"He has his reasons. I'm sure you will figure them out soon enough once you start working with him."

"Am I allowed to know anything about this guy before I fly seven hours to meet him?"

"Mr. Spruce wants to open a rare bookshop in New England. I need you to convince him now is the time to do it. And that Boston is the place to do it."

"He's a billionaire. Is it that difficult to buy a bookstore?"

"It is if you want to do it the right way. He put the rare bookshop plans on hold when his parents passed. It was their dream more than his."

"How do you know all this, Mr. Director?"

"Pierce Spruce is my godson."

"Are you kidding me? How?"

"Knowing the answer to that question is in no way related to this operation, special agent."

"Understood, sir. So, Pierce Spruce is going to be my partner on *Operation Counter Response*?"

"That's my hope. As long as you can convince him to come."

"Let's say I can convince him. How is he supposed to help me?"

"Pierce has connections to *The Response*. His father was in the Royal

Navy with Archie Neville. They were also in Parliament together."

"Does he have any experience in our line of work? Was he ex-military or anything?"

"No. His background is in art history. He has a wide range of knowledge of historical monuments and artifacts. I think more recently, he has been working on becoming a novelist. But we haven't spoken a lot lately."

"And you want me to trust a billionaire art historian with my life?"

"I'm just saying I want you to meet with him and make that decision for yourself. Pierce Spruce has a few things we currently lack on this operation—resources and connections. Simple as that."

"Simple as that? Nothing is ever simple with this job, but I guess I do serve at your pleasure, Mr. Director. I'll be ready to fly to London whenever you want to send me."

"Thank you. I appreciate it, special agent. That will be all."

One

Ring...ring...ring...

"Hello, this is Lucy."

"I'm looking for Pierce—is he around?"

"One moment."

"Pierce, someone is on the phone for you."

I wasn't sure who would be calling or how this person got a hold of our room number. All I knew was I was just getting into my book, the first volume of *Marlborough* by Winston Churchill. I hope that whoever was on the other end of the phone knew that they were interrupting serious business.

"Pierce, please take the phone."

"Do you know who it is?"

"No idea."

We've only been married for a few days, certainly not long enough for Lucy to recognize all of my acquaintances' voices over the phone. Which these days was a pretty small circle, other than the occasional check-in from one of my parents' old friends.

"Hello. This is Pierce."

"Pierce, I'm glad I got a hold of you, and I apologize, I recognize that I'm catching you on your honeymoon."

I immediately knew who was on the line once I heard the voice come through the phone. It was the director of the FBI calling from Washington, DC, a close friend of my late father.

"Good morning, Mr. Director."

"How's married life treating you so far?"

"Fine, sir. Except for you tracking me down on my honeymoon."

Lucy and I had a small ceremony at a cathedral in Paris. The director didn't make the invite list.

"I know. I know. I didn't want to bother you, Pierce, I need your help, though."

Unlike 99% of the world, I wasn't surprised that the director of the FBI tracked down the phone number for my hotel room in Paris, but I was surprised that he was calling me for help. It had been a few years since we last spoke. I assumed he was calling to apologize.

"What's the favor?"

"Are you sitting down?"

What's he about to tell me that would require me to be seated?

"Yes, I am. What's going on?"

"I need your help with a crisis. There's a rogue group that's stealing historical monuments and artifacts from the United States. For example, we have reason to believe that they're plotting to steal the *Constitution*."

"From the National Archives in DC? Good luck with that. That place is a fortress. How do you know that's what they're after?"

"No, no, Pierce. the USS *Constitution*."

I quickly realized why he wanted my assistance. My mother came from a long line of Boston aristocrats. Her family's fortune was largely amassed in the shipping industry. The Pierce family controlled just about everything that came in or out of the Charlestown Navy Yard. The same Navy Yard where the USS *Constitution* just so happens to reside. This "rogue group" isn't looking for a piece of paper. They're trying to steal one of America's most beloved battleships.

"How do you know that? Who are these people trying to take it?"

"The intelligence is spotty at the moment, but they've recently taken the *Colonel William Prescott* statue from Bunker Hill. Each week they seem to be after larger and larger items in the area. We don't know each member by name, but we know the leader, and that's what has me most concerned. It's also another reason why you're the only person who can help me."

"And who's the leader?"

"Archie Neville."

I may not have any experience in the director's line of work, but I know Boston, and I know Archie Neville. Neville was in the Royal Navy with my father. They fought alongside each other in World War II and were members of Parliament at the same time in the late '50s before my father passed. Since his public service, Neville has been making hundreds of millions as CEO of Europe's largest delivery services company—*Reaction Transport*. Neville was a capable adversary for my father, but an adversary nonetheless.

"So, you need my help because you think I can somehow pull strings at the Charlestown Navy Yard and stop Archie Neville from entering the local waters in Boston?"

"That's part of it. You're certainly the only person who knows both the key players and the places that make up their mission." The director took a pause before clarifying his ask, "I want you to come work for me, Pierce."

I never thought I would hear those words come out of his mouth. Especially, given our disagreements in recent years.

"Mr. Director, with all due respect, I'm no FBI agent. I've never even touched a gun. I really don't think I'm your guy."

"Those skills won't be required, Pierce. I want you to be my *New England Monument Adviser*, you will report to me directly. We'll provide you an agent who has been working on this operation since its inception. His name is Special Agent Robert Graham. He's a good agent and will be with you at all times—keeping you safe. Pierce, what I need you for is your brain, your connections, and the influence you have."

New England Monument Adviser...

"Let's say for some unknown and unlikely reason I agree to help. Are you going to let me do this from London? I have others in my life now that I have to consider."

"Unfortunately, not. We need you in Boston where the heists are taking place."

"Well, Mr. Director. I don't know what to say other than I'll need time to think about this and talk it over with Lucy. You understand?"

"I understand. We do need to know sooner rather than later, though, Pierce. When do you return to London?"

"A week from tomorrow."

"I'm going to send Special Agent Graham to come to meet you at your place in London. Unless, of course, you want him to join you in Paris?"

"Yeah, right! Fine. I'll meet him next week at our place in London. But please know this is just a courtesy—I'm not committing to anything."

"Understood."

"Good bye, Mr. Director."

I hung up the phone. Lucy was staring at me in a way that indicated she had caught at least a few bits and pieces of my phone call.

Not sure how I was going to explain this one.

Two

I met Lucy about five years ago on her 26th Birthday. She's ten years younger than I am, and it shows to this day as her face has few wrinkles and curled auburn hair reflects the streaks of light that bounce off of it. Whereas my face has lines that have deepened over the past four decades, and when light bounces off my hair, it illuminates specks of gray.

On the night we met, I was out for a quick drink at a local London bar near my place. Lucy was at the bar with some friends. She was wearing a yellow floral summer dress that swayed back and forth in the areas that didn't cling tightly to her athletic figure. She walked over to talk to me while waiting for her drink. I assumed she wanted to know about the book I was reading—*The Furies* by John Jakes. An American novelist who was writing a series about the United States bicentennial. *Maybe she had read Jakes?* I thought to myself when she first approached. Although, I doubted anyone else in London thought as much of John Jakes writing as I did, if at all. Nor did I imagine any of my fellow Londoners cared to celebrate the American bicentennial.

My interest in it stemmed from my familial roots in Boston. Plus, the writing was spectacular, and since I fancied myself a budding novelist, I figured I could learn a thing or two from the series that was flying off the shelves in the States.

Whether she was interested in my book or not had not concerned me as much as hoping the reason she wanted to meet me was not because she recognized me from the papers. My fear with any female acquaintance was that they would just be another one of those people who only knew me as the son of the famous British banker and politician William Spruce and New England shipping heiress Ophelia Pierce. This was the exact reason I didn't keep many female acquaintances around. I was sick of hearing the same stories told to me by random people who thought they knew something about me based on what they had read. Tabloids that painted me as a reclusive playboy—a degenerate who added nothing to society. Thankfully, Lucy was far from one of these types, and I realized this within the first few minutes of speaking with her that warm summer night. Things seemed so much simpler back when we first started dating. I knew the public exposure that came with my life was not easy for her to adjust to, but she always did her best to make it work. This situation with the FBI was going to take a whole other level of patience and understanding, though.

"Who was that, Pierce?" Lucy asked.

"It was the FBI director."

Lucy had been in my life long enough at this point to know that my relationship with the director was at best complicated.

"What did he want? It's been a while since I've even heard you mention him."

"Nothing. Are you ready to go check out some museums?" I tried to change the subject.

"Pierce, we aren't going anywhere until we talk. Why would the director need to call you in the middle of our honeymoon? Especially when he hasn't reached out in years."

"It's nothing you need to be concerned about."

"I'm your wife now. I'm concerned about everything," Lucy snapped.

"Okay. The director was calling because he needs my help."

"Keep going…"

"He wants me to help stop some bad people from doing some terrible things."

"Why does he need you, though?"

"Because I know the leader of the bad people, and I know a lot about the place he's trying to harm. I don't know much more than that at this point."

"How do you know the leader? Why is the FBI involved? Shouldn't it be MI5 or Scotland Yard?"

"Archie Neville. They aren't attacking London. They're planning to steal monuments from the United States. Boston is their location of choice at the moment."

"The same Archie Neville I see in the papers? Why, Boston?"

"Yeah, the same Archie Neville you see in the papers. He's a successful businessman now, but he used to be in the Royal Navy with my father. They were also in Parliament together. My mother's ancestors used to have a lot of important connections around Boston. Back when they controlled most of the ports throughout New England. That's why he thinks I can help. But, I still have a lot of questions."

"So, when do we go?"

"Go where?"

"Boston," Lucy said as she pushed curls of hair out of her eyes.

"We don't need to go to Boston. We don't need to help at all if we don't want to. Working for the FBI in any capacity is dangerous. Plus, we haven't even moved your things into the townhouse in London. I don't want to talk about this on our honeymoon. Maybe once we get back, we can talk more about it."

"I'm not saying you should do it. I'm just saying you made your decision. I can see it in your eyes. I could tell by the way your voice quivered on the phone. You already made your choice, so I might as well keep my bags packed and get ready to move to Boston."

"Can we just enjoy the rest of the honeymoon, please? I just want to check out some museums and walk around Paris. Let's try to have some fun this week before even discussing what the director said."

"Well, that should be easy, considering you haven't told me anything the director said to you."

"Exactly."

I reached over the nightstand and traded my book for my wedding band and Cartier Tank watch.

"Come on. Time to go to the *Louvre*," I said.

"Only if you promise me we'll be talking about this later, Pierce."

"Of course, dear."

My conversation with the director came up a few times, but it remained a superficial one. I insisted that we wait for our return to London before getting serious about the content of the phone call. Unfortunately for me, that day arrived faster than I'd hoped. We flew back early Monday morning, both of us exhausted from a week of exploring France. The black driving car pulled in front of our London gray-stone townhouse. It belonged to me in the past, but now it was ours. We had the rest of our lives ahead of us and could not be more excited. However, I was still contemplating my call with the director and couldn't help but think about how that may change things and how soon he would follow up regarding Archie Neville's "rogue group" of thieves. I wondered how many days it would be until he sent his agent over to visit me. I quickly got an answer to that question because as I continued my walk to the front door of the townhouse, I could see that another driving car similar to the one we were just in was waiting across the street.

"Is that one of the neighbors?" Lucy asked.

A tall, athletic-looking black man with a closely cropped afro and large framed glasses exited the vehicle and made his way to our doorstep. He was a man I'd never seen before, but I suspected by the looks of the cheap suit and tie on this hot summer day that the director sent him. We set down our bags on the front steps and prepared to greet our guest, but he got the first word.

"Are you Mr. Spruce?" He asked.

"I am. Can I help you with something?"

"My name is Special Agent Robert Graham. I was sent by the FBI director to come to meet with you about our current dilemma in

Boston," he said.

I gave Lucy a look, indicating I was equally surprised to see our guest so soon. We assumed the director would at least give us a day to settle back in. I was kind of hoping in the back of my mind that the whole thing may just blow over entirely, and we would never have an agent show up at our doorstep. So much for that optimistic thinking.

"We just got back from our honeymoon. I suppose the director didn't mention that part? Let me put down these bags and shower really quick. After that, we can meet in my study. Can I fix you a drink?" I asked.

"I can't drink on the job, Mr. Spruce. Thank you for being willing to let me into your home on such short notice," Special Agent Robert Graham responded.

"Not a problem. I've known the director for a long time and figured he wouldn't waste a minute. I insist you have a drink if you would like one, though. I haven't agreed to anything, so I don't think you should consider this a working meeting. Just two new acquaintances talking over a drink."

"Maybe we can start slow with coffee or something. In the meantime, I'm happy to help with these bags."

Special Agent Graham grabbed Lucy's bags. She smiled and gladly handed them over.

"Such a gentleman, thank you. I wish my husband would take some notes."

I rolled my eyes and left it at that.

Once inside the townhouse, I grabbed a bottle of whiskey and some of the Queen's preferred bitters, mixing them with a few splashes of water and two sugar cubes before stirring in the whiskey. I dropped in an ice cube and an orange peel and left Special Agent Graham in the study accompanied by his drink. I figured it was up to him whether or not he wanted to indulge.

"Feel free to look around the study and take whatever you'd like off the shelves. I just ordered a multi-volume biography on Churchill—I will need the extra shelf space to accommodate upon its arrival," I said as I exited the study to go wash up.

Three

"You have a lot of interesting books, Mr. Spruce. I wish I could say I've read more of them. I find it hard to read as much as I know I should. Just no time in my schedule, I guess."

"What kinds of books do you like to read, Agent Graham?" I asked as I shook some water off my hair that was left over from the shower.

"Biographies and memoirs, if I had to choose. It looks like you have a nice collection of those."

"I do, and other genres as well, but I too love a good biography. Do you have any favorites?"

"Sports biographies mainly. I grew up wanting to be a baseball player, not exactly the direction my career has gone so far, but who knows, maybe my big break is still to come."

"Who's your favorite baseball player?" I asked as if I knew any.

"Nowadays? I don't know if I have one. The FBI has been giving me a lot of special assignments lately—which hasn't left a lot of time to watch baseball. I grew up in Brooklyn—so Jackie Robinson has always been a favorite."

I felt terrible I didn't have any baseball books I could give to the special agent. Sports was one area where I was much more British than American. I assumed that he didn't have much interest in reading about the history of Polo. I made a quick note on the canary legal pad sitting on my desk.

Order biography on Jackie Robinson—Brooklyn.

Special Agent Graham spoke back up before I could apologize for the shortcoming of my library.

"The director said you're quite the collector of rare books."

"Yeah, I have a decent amount. All of my rare books have various bindings, editions, and a few are signed, but not many. My collection is nothing like some people I've seen over the years. My father took me to Chartwell once, and there were some incredible books there that I could only dream of getting my hands on."

"You like Churchill, huh?"

"He was a friend of my grandfather. I think he's a very underrated writer. I assume you didn't come here to talk about books or Churchill, though."

"Not entirely."

"What are you here for?"

"Well, I know you've been briefed about our concerns in Boston, correct?"

"That's right. The director warned me that some group led by Archie Neville took the statue of *Colonel Prescott* from Bunker Hill and now they have their eyes on taking the USS *Constitution*?"

"Correct. Did he tell you what he wants you to do for us in Boston?"

"No, he didn't. He truly wants me to make this trip right when I am starting a family?"

"Yes, he does. He wants you to come to Boston and bring all of these fine books with you. The director wants you to start a bookshop as a front for what you'll actually be doing there—which will be helping me stop *The Response* before they cause more damage."

"*The Response*? Is that what they call themselves?"

"Yes, that's right."

"Unbelievable."

21

"What's that?"

"He's taking advantage of me. The director knows that my parent's dream was to spend half the year in the U.S. and start a museum containing their library of rare books and paintings."

"Correct, the director's hoping if, for no other reason, you'll do this for your parents…" The special agent took a brief pause before continuing with questions, "what do you say, Mr. Spruce? Will you come to be the director's New England Monument Adviser?"

I didn't want to be selfish. I fully recognized that I needed to let Lucy be a part of this decision, but it would be difficult to convince me not to accept Agent Graham's offer after hearing what I had heard. Even though Lucy and I had only had limited conversations about the topic—I was confident that she appreciated why I had to do this. I just needed to hear her say it aloud. No one else had the knowledge necessary to help out the FBI director and Special Agent Graham in the same ways I could. If nothing else, they would need resources in order to stop Neville. Resources they must not have currently, or else they wouldn't be in this situation. They knew that with me on board—they would always have a blank check.

The door opened a crack.

"Pierce. Can I get you and Special Agent Graham anything?" Lucy asked as she came into the study.

Lucy had a way of turning heads when entering a room. Her hair was still wet from the shower, having just cleaned up from the long flight. Even in a shirt and jeans, there was no hiding her athletic build. She was a swimmer at University and maintained her competitive shape much better than I did these days. Granted, I was a polo player—not a swimmer. But what was even more impressive than her beauty was her mind. Unfortunately, people usually had to spend a few days with her before realizing how special that part of her was.

"No, thank you. I think we are set for the moment," I said.

Lucy was just about to walk out the door when I decided I needed to keep my vow that I would include her in every aspect of my life. Especially in a situation like this where I knew Lucy's brains would benefit the FBI should we agree to come to Boston. The experience she gained while working at the financial firm in London was indispensable. Dealing with London's wealthiest businessmen and being able to call them out when she disagreed with their decision-making was something that would be of great value at some point during the operation, I was sure.

"Lucy, I need to talk to you about something. Special Agent Graham has asked for our help and…" Before I could finish, Lucy cut me off.

"If we're moving to Boston—I want to pick the place where we will live. You have no idea what to look for in a home."

She left the room. She didn't know what she was signing up for, but I guess she knew me well enough to realize I wasn't going to turn down the opportunity to help out an old friend of my father's. No matter how upset I had been with him since he took over as director of the FBI.

My three main hesitations were—Lucy's opinion on the move, the risk level of the operation, and the fact that I hadn't been to New England since someone killed my parents there just 20 years ago.

"Sounds like Mrs. Spruce is on board. How about you, Mr. Spruce?"

I tipped my glass towards Agent Graham, "tell me more about *The Response*."

Four

Although my main concern was how Lucy felt about me working for the director—I was also concerned about my own safety. I lived a pretty sheltered childhood. My parents and nannies raised me on a large estate outside of London in Buckinghamshire. The estate was expansive and included almost forty rooms. Various forms of wild game surrounded the Tudor mansion. Animals of all forms, birds, sheep, horses, deer, and dogs, of course. I loved the fresh air but didn't care for hunting. The estate gave me a childhood full of fond memories. There were, of course, a few negatives that came with this lifestyle. I often lacked close contact with other children. Being an only child with 4,000 acres to roam was not always the best for socializing with others. My isolated situation drove me deeper into books. Through my reading, I built relationships with brave individuals, hero's through the centuries. Even though I was often alone, I swear I could feel their presence from time to time when I read outside in the pastures or inside my father's study.

"Agent Graham, another round before we dive into all this?" I asked even though the special agent hadn't had a sip of his first drink.

"No thank you, Mr. Spruce."

"Suit yourself, Agent Graham. Hope you don't mind if I have a second old fashioned."

"It's your home, Mr. Spruce. You do what you need to do."

"I don't need it. I want it; I make a good old fashioned and deserve to make a few more before I sell this place."

"What do you mean?"

"I mean, I'm going to have another old fashioned."

"No, not that. You said you were going to sell this place?"

"Well yeah, if I'm moving to Boston—then I may as well sell it."

"Why would you do that? Not to be forward, Mr. Spruce, but you aren't hurting for cash. You could easily keep all of your real estate here in London. No matter how long you're in Boston."

Not sure how much I need to tell Agent Graham about my past when we had so much work to do regarding the future. I decided not to tell him why I sold all of my family's real estate. I suppose there are times when I kind of like the fact that people tend to think of me as the degenerate son of a prestigious family—it means that I can only surprise people for the better if they meet me in person. The tabloids claim I sold the houses for my own personal gain. But they have no clue what I actually did with that money.

"I guess I can hang on to it for a little longer. I may need the extra storage. There's no way I will be able to move every single book to New England right away. It sounds like I just need to find a place in Boston, so I can help get this mess taken care of before it gets worse."

"The FBI is happy to find you a place in Charlestown—or elsewhere in Boston if you prefer. We owe you something for helping us out, and we can't pay you a salary since this needs to stay off the books."

"Give me a break. The FBI can't afford anything that would be able to hold a quarter of my rare book collection. At least, not with their recent budget cuts."

"Alright, well, don't say I didn't offer. I guess we should get to work. If you're going to commit to moving your family, you should know what you're signing up for," Agent Graham said as he pulled out his strategy binder. The spine of it read "*Operation Counter Response.*"

My original assumption was that they knew close to nothing about *The Response*, but to my surprise, based on the size of this binder, they had been able to collect at least some valuable information. That fact put my nerves at ease—for now, at least.

"Alright, let's start at the top. You know Archie Neville and his background, obviously, Admiral in the Royal Navy, Member of Parliament, CEO of a European transport company, and so on. The key is that Archie Neville is the descendant of a handful of prominent British military personnel. One of which was a senior officer who died during the Revolutionary War."

"Which battle?" I asked.

"Bunker Hill," Agent Graham answered.

That's interesting. My great, great, great, great grandfather Oliver "Ollie" Pierce also fought at Bunker Hill. On the opposing side of Neville's ancestor, of course, but Neville's ancestor was on the same side as my other great, great, great, great grandfather Samuel Spruce. I was always curious if my ancestors met on the hill, Bunker or Breed's or wherever, but now I wanted to know if either of them knew Neville's ancestor.

"So, that's why he's interested in Boston?" I asked.

"That seems to be the only logical connection. During our intelligence gathering, we learned that Archie's great grandfather was determined to see a Neville become Prime Minister and end the alliance with the United States. We aren't sure precisely why that was his goal—but safe to say he had revenge on his mind."

"Explains why no one ever wanted a Neville to be Prime Minister."

"Exactly. But clearly that plan hasn't panned out. Bringing us now to Archie, who at 74 years old, seems to have a different kind of revenge in mind—the stealing of monuments."

"There's got to be more to it than that. Neville's ancestors died centuries ago, and it sounds like mainly in battle. Battles they volunteered to fight in. He might be upset about what happened, but there's bound to be more to it, right?"

"I agree with you, Mr. Spruce. But I have limited resources at my disposal. So, I have had to focus almost exclusively on the more pressing "what" and "when" questions. Perhaps with you on board, we can start to figure out the "why."

"And you believe the "what" is the USS *Constitution*?" I asked.

"Neville has been seen in Boston quite a bit lately. His company *Reaction Transport* has been very active shipping crates in and out of the nearby ports. This is why we started looking into it more. Then once the statue of *Colonel Prescott* disappeared the same night a *Reaction Transport* boat left the harbor—we knew that all but confirmed our fears about Neville."

I hadn't heard the stories about Neville's family before, but that didn't matter. I still never trusted him. Every time I crossed the man, which luckily wasn't often, he always gave off an aura that he was hiding something. He would constantly whisper to the people around him, and those people would never talk to anyone but Neville. I may have been young the last time I was around him, but I had attended enough high society events to know that Neville didn't behave like everyone else. No hugs, no kisses on the cheek, no handshakes, no interaction at all. He would just watch people and whisper to his henchman.

I could always trust my father's instincts. My father was the type of man who liked or at least got along with just about everyone. However, when I saw him around Archie Neville, I could tell that he had a problem with him. A snarl always appeared on my father's lip when he was in Neville's presence—something I'd never witnessed with anyone else throughout my childhood.

"Why not just protect the ship? Can't you put the Navy or Coast Guard on the case and just have them surround the *Constitution*?" I asked.

"We thought about that, but there are a few issues. If we protect the *Constitution*—they'll simply divert their efforts to the next monument on the list. The second problem is the government has asked that we keep this off the books—mainly because the president doesn't want to pay for it with taxpayer dollars. No one knows about *The Response* except you, me, the director, the president, and a small team of analysts back at the Bureau."

"Do we know much about the rest of *The Response* outside of

Neville? I'm curious how he gets people to do this stuff."

"Neville's right-hand man is the young talented former Lieutenant-Commander Toby Morgan. He's silently taking the lead on recruiting and training new members. All known members of *The Response* have day jobs at *Reaction Transport*. Every employee at *Reaction Transport* is ex-military from various countries. Neville's found the best of the best and provided them an opportunity to succeed in the business world—along with healthy "bonuses" based on the company's financial statements we got."

"How did you get your hands on those?"

"You don't want to know. But I'll tell you that Reaction Transport's security at their London offices aren't big fans of mine."

Agent Graham was right—I didn't want to know what he did to get those reports. But, I didn't need an explanation to appreciate that having him on my side for protection would be an asset for me.

"So, what's our first move? How do you even begin to approach a special operation like this?"

Like this. As if I knew how to approach any kind of special operation.

"The first move is to get you and Lucy to Boston and set up the rare bookshop."

"How's starting a bookshop even going to help us?"

"The bookshop will solidify why you're in town. The last thing we want is for *The Response* to know that you're aware of their presence. In the same vein, you're one of the most mysterious billionaires in the world, and a lot of people in New England will be intrigued by any business that your name is attached to."

"Archie Neville certainly won't be "interested" in my being in Boston. Aren't you concerned about that?"

"Not really. He is busy running an international business after all. He probably won't find out about you being in Boston for a few days at least, and even when he does, we're going to make the bookshop a tribute to your mother's family—so it won't be odd that you're in town to open things up. Neville won't know you're in town because of him."

I thought about pushing back on using my parent's likeness as an advantage for any of this, but it did make sense. I figured my parents would at least be proud to know that their dream of starting a rare bookshop in New England would be coming to fruition.

"Alright. That works for me."

"Good. So, the plan is to leave this time next week, which will give you a week to get your affairs in order. We'll send movers for your things—especially the books."

"Okay. That works. I do have a few stipulations if I'm going to do this, though."

"What would those be? I'm sure we can work out whatever arrangement would make things easiest on you and Lucy."

"I would like to pick the location of the bookshop if that's okay with the Bureau. Since we want to be close to the Bunker Hill Monument and the USS *Constitution*, I assume it would be easiest to be in Charlestown, which should work well for Lucy and me. What would you think about living in the same building as us? We could have the shop on the first floor, and you could take the top floor. I thought we could find a walk-up with four floors altogether. I hope to put the bookshop on the bottom floor, Lucy and I on the second floor, the study on the third, and your living space on top. Lucy and I will plan to buy the whole walk-up, and you can live there free of charge if you're up for it. I think this set-up will help us have constant communication that will be required if we're going to be successful."

"Are you sure that's what you want? The FBI typically covers my living expenses—you don't have to do this if you don't want to," Agent Graham said.

"Yes, I want to. I don't believe the Bureau should be paying for anything that isn't your salary or that they don't have to. You might work for the federal government, but you also work with me at *Pierce's Rare Books on Bunker Hill*."

"You already have a name, huh? I like it."

"That's what my mom would have liked, as well. If we're going to honor her, we may as well choose the name she would've wanted."

"I agree. Well, I think that's pretty much it for now. I don't want to overload you with information until we're all settled in Boston."

"Shouldn't we get started now? That's a large binder you have there.

I assume there's more for me to learn?"

"The less you know now—the better—at least until we get you to Boston. I wouldn't want you to back out."

I tipped my glass towards Agent Graham in agreement. He exited the study without saying another word.

"So, what did you learn?" Lucy asked as she entered the room following the special agent's abrupt departure.

"Enough."

"Enough? What does that even mean?"

"Enough that I'm convinced I need to make a trip out to Boston."

"You mean we need to make a trip to Boston."

"But I haven't even given you all the details yet."

"I don't need all the details right now. I heard enough of your conversation to understand why you feel compelled to go. If you're convinced, then I'm right there with you."

We began packing my things and anything Lucy wanted to bring from the townhouse.

So much for settling into our comfortable life in London.

Five

The past week had gone by quickly. It took a lot of time to make sure our things could safely make it to Boston—especially the books and my parents' art collection. Sitting on the plane now waiting to depart the private airport was the first time I was able to take a breath and try to wrap my head around what we were doing moving to Boston.

"Are you nervous about going back?" Lucy asked as she took her hand and pushed back my thick head of black and gray hair that tended to stand up on planes. It must've been something with the way the air circulates in planes or the lack of air circulating. I wasn't sure.

"Honestly?" I asked.

"Yeah, Pierce. I always expect honesty."

"Yes. I'm nervous. I have barely been able to sleep at night. I loved New England as a kid, but that feels like a lifetime ago now."

"Anyone in your situation would be nervous. You should just be proud that you're trying to do what's right. That's what matters."

"It only matters if we're successful," I said.

The plane was about to go wheels up. I brought out a Herman

31

Wouk novel I had started the night before that I thought would keep my mind off things during the flight. It was somewhat successful, but I could still feel my stomach churning as we took off. It didn't go away for the first hour or so of the flight, if at all. I only ever flew in my family's private plane, so you would think that I would be able to get comfortable and relax, but that never seemed to be the case. I could only get through a few pages at a time without feeling symptoms of dizziness. I tried to stand up and walk around the plane, but nothing worked. Nothing ever worked.

I sat back in my seat and clutched a pillow over my eyes.

"Do you think your father would have ever tried to become Prime Minister?" Lucy asked.

"No, I don't think so," I muffled through the pillow.

"Did your father ever talk to you about running for Parliament? I think you would do a good job," Lucy said.

I had no interest in getting involved in politics. The world had more than enough politicians and not enough novelists. At least, that's how I felt. Others probably disagreed.

"I don't know about that—I don't think I have the stomach for politics. I can barely keep my nerves on this flight. I just hope I can finish my novel someday, that's the only personal achievement I care about," I said.

"Why are you doing this then?"

"Doing what?"

"About to put your life on the line for a country, and you aren't even a citizen. Why do it?"

It was a good question. I was proud of my heritage but had never considered that I wasn't even a dual citizen. Spending so much time in New England growing up, I felt like a dual citizen in my heart, but no piece of paper confirmed that. Perhaps, the director could help me take care of that at the end of my mission. My hands were starting to shake slightly, but I couldn't tell if it was nerves or turbulence.

"Just feel the need to help out—I guess. The director is a dear family friend, and it just seems like the right thing to do given my connections to both him and New England."

I knew there was more to it than just a favor for the director, but I wasn't in the mood to dig any deeper and hoped Lucy wouldn't either. She seemed to be pondering the answer but fell asleep before she could follow up. I have no idea how she slept on planes. She didn't even fly much before we met. Staying calm on planes, nonetheless, being able to sleep on them, was a skill that I've never had. To me, this flight, in particular, felt like one of the bumpiest rides I had ever experienced. It had been 20 years since I'd flown across the Atlantic, and planes were much more reliable now. The Spruce family jet was remarkably safe, but my hands were still shaking as I attempted to take a sip of my drink. The whiskey on this flight was high quality; at least, I could always count on that. It was one of the few perks of owning a plane that never really got used. I still kicked around the idea of selling it, but ultimately it was worth it to keep. I hoped that Lucy would make more use of it than I had the past few decades. The plane was currently reminding me of all the reasons I preferred short flights to other European countries when I had to fly. The less time in the air—the better.

A few more restless hours went by before we landed. London is five hours ahead of Boston, so we were slightly jet-lagged when we arrived. It would surely get even worse over the next few nights as we attempted to adjust our sleep schedules. Regardless of how we felt physically, we had a lot of work to do. The first order of business was choosing our new home. We were able to get pictures of three housing options in Charlestown in advance of arrival—so we had a sense of what to expect.

After what was a long, painful flight, the plane finally came to a complete stop. A car and driver were there waiting patiently for our arrival. We climbed in the car, and I took out the details about each walk-up to go through with Lucy as we drove to the first option. About 15 to 20 minutes passed before the driver dropped us off in front of walk-up number one. It was a brick building with four levels. It was tucked between the Bunker Hill Monument, where *The Response* recently removed the statue of *Colonel William Prescott*, and The Training Field, upon which stands a statue of a woman "America" who watches over a Union soldier and sailor. The Training Field received its name for the countless colonial militia that were trained there in preparation for battle.

The statue commemorates not just the soldiers who were developed there but the thousands of others from Charlestown who fought for worthy causes. With both Bunker Hill and the Training Field being home to Charlestown's finest monuments—it seemed an appropriate location to start the bookshop.

As soon as we stepped out of the car, Lucy said this was the one she wanted. I encouraged her to check out the other options knowing there were some other nice places, but she had no interest in looking any further. She was confident this was the perfect location for her new home. I was amazed by the poise she had shown this past week. Although, after all these years, I suppose it was a trait that should no longer surprise me. It was just part of who she was. Yet, she continued to leave me speechless. I mean, there can't be that many women in the world that would jump on board with their new husband deciding to work a special operation for the FBI. I married the right person. Having never had a traditional day job, I tended to do things on a whim. For example, I may wake up in the morning and want to spend my entire day in a museum—in which case I do just that. On the other hand, if I want to head to a cottage on the English countryside and read for a week straight or attempt to work on my novel, then without hesitation—I do it. This took a little getting used to for Lucy, who did her best to keep her 9-5 job at the finance firm for as long as she could, but eventually, keeping up with my flights of fancy forced her to leave the firm and do financial consulting on a client by client basis. So far, it hadn't strained our relationship, but this latest adventure was taking it to another level, even for me.

I could tell right away that Lucy was falling in love with Boston's beauty. The walk-up we decided on had a clear view from all levels of The Bunker Hill Monument, a testament to a battle fought long ago in the summer of 1775. The American rebels lost this particular battle, but they fought valiantly enough to give the people faith that they could win the war for independence. Today, the battle is honored by a large granite obelisk that has stood on the hill since the 1800s.

Directly in front of the monument was the proper home of a man wielding his sword for the revolution. That man—Colonel William Prescott. Prescott led the defense of the hill from the invading British soldiers. His troops fought off multiple assaults by British forces but soon ran out of their already limited supplies. Colonel Prescott was one of the last to leave the hill after the colonial militia's ammo had run dry. The Colonel had to fight his way through the British forces to safety using only his sword. Hence why Prescott's sword is such an iconic piece of the statue today. However, if someone visited the site on this day, all they would see was a concrete slab that served as the statue's base. It was one thing to hear about the impact *The Response's* actions were going to have, but when I saw the Bunker Hill Monument with no *Colonel Prescott* statue to protect it, I could now see firsthand the effect of *The Response*.

Aside from the beautiful monuments and surrounding parks that luckily remained—Lucy and I also enjoyed what we saw on the inside of our new home. Architecture from the middle of the 19th Century reminded me of my childhood. The place had slight internal resemblances to my grandparents' homes, both the estate in Newport, Rhode Island, and the townhouse in Beacon Hill. Of course, the Newport home was much more opulent, but I still felt some similarities when I saw the crystal chandeliers that the prior owners had hung. I guess I always felt guilty knowing it was because of me that my family had since sold the Newport and Beacon Hill properties. Some years ago, my grandparents assumed I, the only grandchild, would not use them. This was wise on their end, I suppose, considering this was my first trip across the pond in two decades. Luckily, we seemed to have found a new home that was just as good as the others—albeit in a new neighborhood. Charlestown residents traditionally belonged to a different socioeconomic class than those of Beacon Hill, but I was quickly finding Charlestown's architecture and character just as appealing. The home met all of our criteria. As long as Agent Graham was on board—then the place was a go.

Agent Graham met up with us about 45 minutes after we arrived in Charlestown. He wondered why we were still at the first housing option until he noticed that Lucy was already unpacking books.

"You picked a place already? You must've checked out the other options pretty quickly?" He asked.

"Nope. Lucy just walked into this one and started unpacking. Do you have any issues with it? I wanted to get your opinion on how you like the fourth floor before I committed."

"Mr. Spruce. I grew up in a studio apartment in Brooklyn. My bedroom was a pull-out couch. My mother raised me alone. I'm pretty sure any place that suits you fine will be the nicest place I'll live in my entire life."

"At least go check out the fourth floor first. I want to make sure you like it."

"If that would make you happy Mr. Spruce, then I'll go check it out."

Agent Graham began walking up the old wooden stairs.

While Agent Graham was upstairs, I continued to unload books with Lucy. I worked on separating my personal books for the study from what would be on the shelves in the bookshop. I didn't bring my whole collection, but I must have taken about 700 books from my library in London based on the number of boxes still left to unpack. I realized that the bookshop was just a cover, but I wanted it to be a respectable business. The world needs more quality rare bookshops, and I planned to give it another. As I pulled books out of boxes, I found myself allowing for much more of my personal library to be available for purchase than I had initially anticipated. However, I did put aside a few stacks that I absolutely could not sell. These stacks consisted of volumes that generations of my family had passed down. One stack also included my father's signed manuscript of *Why England Slept* by John F. Kennedy. A book that started as President Kennedy's senior thesis at Harvard and took a critical look at the British government's delayed action leading up to World War II.

It was a binding of the original manuscript for the book and was my most prized possession. With that and a few dozen others set aside—I decided that most everything else would be available for the public to enjoy. The overflow would be kept in the study, where I planned to have a more controlled chamber of shelving units put in to help provide the environment required for the oldest and rarest of the books to survive. The books wouldn't have price tags. I would decide the cost on a book-by-book basis based on how much the work meant to the buyer and make a final decision regarding the price at that time. My goal wasn't to make money selling books—I had more than enough money—I just wanted the books to bring joy to people. That's what my ancestors desired when they bought most of these books in the first place.

We soon settled in for the evening after what was a long day, and opened a bottle of wine. I finally had the chance to gather myself. It was in this quiet moment that I realized I was back where I belonged.

Six

"Pierce, wake up," Lucy said as she gave my shoulder a shove, "do you want to go for a walk or something? I can't sleep."

It was the best night of sleep I had had in a few weeks. Nothing could stop me from catching up on some much-needed rest, nothing except my wife, apparently.

"Sure, honey, but I'm going to need to shower first. Then maybe we can take a walk to the Navy Yard."

"Okay, well get moving then." Lucy pushed my shoulder again.

I took a quick cold shower to get a jolt of energy. It was already a balmy 85 degrees even this early in the morning. Boston may have been humid this time of year, but its beauty was striking and made the sticky sweat that accompanied being outside worth it. We got dressed and walked the few blocks to the Navy Yard, where you could get a sense of the city skyline.

The Navy Yard had some of the best views in the city, and of course, was the current residence of the USS *Constitution*. A few of my ancestors were involved with overseeing the ship's building in Boston's

North End, just a quick walk across the bridge from the Navy Yard.

Originally commissioned by President George Washington to fight off pirates—the USS *Constitution*'s fate changed course during the War of 1812 when she had to partake in a few battles. All of which she survived.

Nowadays, the USS *Constitution* serves as a floating tribute to the past. The Navy Yard itself, like the historic ship, isn't as active as it once was. However, there's still a large, much more active pier across the water that serves as a headquarters for the U.S. Coast Guard and their numerous powerboats—which are most commonly used to chase down drug smugglers. Quite the opposite of the piers on the Charlestown side that mainly hosts retired Naval ships, fancy yachts, and dinghy sailboats. All of which are docked just in front of about a mile of old brick buildings. Buildings that had they been abandoned anywhere outside of New England—would have been torn down and replaced decades ago.

Since the Navy Yard is no longer "active," it now plays a largely ceremonial role. Even so, it is still maintained by the Navy—along with the help of the National Park Services. Between the Coast Guard, Navy, and National Park Rangers, I was hoping Agent Graham and I would be allowed to loop someone in to help us out. But the president was worried that if the sailors and park rangers knew about *The Response*, they would try to get involved and potentially be in harm's way. That's what Agent Graham mentioned to me at least. The threat of losing a sailor or park ranger, and at the same time, bringing public exposure to *The Response* were both things the president wanted to avoid.

"I like it here. At least so far. There's actually room on the sidewalks to walk for once," Lucy said as she strolled and gazed at the boats bobbing in the water.

Even though it was still a busy place, Charlestown was not nearly as crowded as our neighborhood in London. Plus, this early in the morning, only the most dedicated walkers and joggers were roaming. Regardless, I was glad Lucy felt this way. She had never traveled outside of Europe before now. So, it was a relief that she liked Boston so far.

"Is that the ship over there?" Lucy asked.

She now saw one of the masts that I had had my eyes on for the past few minutes.

"Yes. It is."

"Can we go on it?"

"Not now, probably a little early for the museum to open up. Plus, I wouldn't want anyone to see me over there right now. Not without Agent Graham's go-ahead. Let's just keep walking."

"Was Boston your favorite place to visit growing up?" Lucy asked as she continued to walk in front of me.

"Boston and Newport, Rhode Island were my two favorite places, but those were also the places we went most often. I loved it when I got to go to Paris as well—the flight is a little more tolerable," I answered.

Lucy didn't say anything for a few blocks. I couldn't tell if she was still taking it all in or if she had something on her mind.

"Are we close to where it happened?"

I guess that question confirmed she had something on her mind.

"It happened in Newport. We're probably just over an hour away," I answered.

"Do you want to go to Newport while we're here? Or would that be too difficult for you?"

"No. I'm never going back to Newport."

Neither of us said another word the rest of the walk back to our new temporary home.

Seven

"How's the organizing going?" Agent Graham asked as he joined me in rifling through boxes of books. He came down to the first floor of the townhouse, where the bookshop would be about 30 minutes after Lucy and I returned from our stroll around the Navy Yard.

"So far, so good. You want to help me start getting the shelves ready to go?"

"Sure. Let me ask you a question first, though. Do you drink coffee?"

"Yes, of course. Lucy is brewing some now."

"Okay, good, I'm going to need some before we start. You being a Londoner, I was worried you only drank tea."

"I have my mother's taste buds, I suppose."

"Any thoughts on how you want the place to look?" Agent Graham asked as he grabbed the legal pad that had some of my designs jotted down.

"My thought is we'll have floor-to-ceiling built-ins put in on the back wall. Directly in front of which I'll have my desk. In addition to my desk, there'll be six other large desks set up—two columns of three with a walkway in the middle that leads to my desk in the back. That way, people will come up and speak with me to check out books. I can tell them a little bit about the history of the book itself and its contents. Then the customer can take a look at the book for themselves at a desk of their choosing."

"You want each person to talk to you? They can't just pick up a book like any other library or bookstore?" Agent Graham asked.

"That would be pointless. The customer wouldn't get to know the story of the book itself. If I was worried about selling books—I might do it the traditional way. But since this is my shop, and I don't plan on making a dime off of the business, I might as well run it based on my vision," I answered.

"Suit yourself. Whatever keeps you around to help me out, I'm all for."

"Do you want a desk of your own, Agent Graham?"

"Nope. No one can see me down here. I need to stay behind the scenes."

"How come? You don't want to work for me down here in the bookshop? What do you need? Benefits? A pension? You name it. I'm open to negotiations," I said sarcastically.

"Mr. Spruce. What's the first thing you thought when you saw me on your doorstep in London?"

"I thought you were a federal agent. But in fairness, I was kind of expecting your arrival."

"My point exactly, I don't need *The Response* knowing I exist. I'll leave all bookshop operations to you in the case they show up."

I was starting to get more comfortable joking around, or at least being sarcastic with Agent Graham. He was a little stiff, as you might expect of a federal agent, but he wasn't quite as stiff as most people I've met who work for the government. It made me more excited to work with him. Maybe even get to know him better.

"Okay, so once the bookshelves are put in, and we get some media promotions set up—we'll open up shop? Does that work okay for you?" Agent Graham asked.

"That works on my end. May take a few days."

"Right, within a few days we open the bookshop—we'll want to take it slow at first and make sure to talk to every customer that enters those doors. We need to get a sense of how the Charlestown community is doing. See if anyone has noticed any unusual activity in the Navy Yard," Agent Graham said.

"Do you think we're moving fast enough?"

"This is all part of the process, Mr. Spruce."

"Please just call me Pierce. If we're going to work together, we might as well get more relaxed around one another."

"I don't relax around many people. But if that's better for you then okay. You can't call me by my first name, though. Graham works fine. The analysts usually call me that."

"So, what's the next part of your plan then, Graham?"

"We let them make the first move. We have a big thing going for us, and that's your international name recognition. Regardless of how Archie Neville feels about you, the people that work for him are bound to want to know more about the bookshop. At least one of them will come in. On the other side of the coin—if Neville does find out you're here—he'll likely send someone to see what you're up to. This is exactly what we want. The bookshop bringing *The Response* out of hiding is how its opening will play into our "real" mission," Graham confirmed.

"I'm doubtful any *Response* members will want to come to the bookshop to see me, but they may come after something I have. Maybe one of my rare books is on their list."

"The best thing you can do for us now is get this place up and running," Graham said as he ran his finger across a window sill covered in dust.

"Alright, let me go call a few carpenters about putting in the shelves."

I could hear graceful footsteps coming down the stairs.

"Anyone want coffee?"

"Yes! Thanks so much, Lucy. I would love some coffee." Graham walked across the shop to grab a mug.

"Here you go," Lucy said as she poured the steaming black coffee from the pot. "Pierce, this place is kind of a mess…"

I pulled the final book out of the last remaining moving box.

"I know. I'm working on it. I'm going to give the carpenter a call now."

"Well, get to it. I'm ready to see this place in action," Lucy said as she topped off my coffee mug and went back upstairs to get our personal boxes unpacked.

It sounds like Graham wasn't the only one that wanted me to shape this place up. I grabbed the phone and started dialing the carpenter.

There was work to be done.

Eight

The carpenters arrived that afternoon and began to work on the new bookshelves. Meanwhile, I took my things and went up to the third-floor study to work on some writing. My writing for the day was mainly focused on journaling about my experiences back in Boston so far. It was nice to have a few moments to be alone with my thoughts. But, unfortunately, I didn't have enough time, or maybe enough energy, to work on the writing that I really needed to make progress on—the manuscript for my first novel. I wish I could say the manuscript was coming along, but with all the wedding planning the past few months, it had taken a backseat. I found it challenging to get back into the story anytime I took even a few days off working on it. And I have been working on it for years at this point. I don't know why but I just can't get it to come together. I go through spurts of great motivation when I will do nothing but chip away at it for days on end, but then I read through it, and I just can't figure out why anyone should care. I guess I care because, in a way, it's about me. The main character lives in an abandoned Scottish castle. A castle he inherited and has now been put in charge of.

Knock...Knock...

"Graham?"

I quickly stashed my writings into my desk and acted like I was unpacking. I didn't want Graham to know I was attempting to write a novel. At least, not yet.

"Yeah it's me. Can I come in?"

"You can let yourself in whenever you want." The door slowly opened as the special agent peeked his head around it.

"Pierce, this is your space. I'm not just going to barge in here," Graham said as he entered through the door that was now fully opened.

"Did you come to help me organize some more books? I'm working my way through the Presidential Papers of Teddy Roosevelt," I said as I grabbed a volume out of the moving box closest to my desk chair. "You being a proud New Yorker, I figured you would be excited."

"Wait, seriously? Teddy Roosevelt wrote these? Believe it or not, the Roosevelt's and the Graham's are two very different kinds of New Yorkers."

Graham picked up one of the volumes that was hanging off of the desk. I had sprawled them out on the large mahogany tabletop to ensure that pages didn't get damaged from the move.

"Yeah, only one year of his presidency, unfortunately. I wish I had more," I said.

"Unfortunately? There's nothing unfortunate about having papers that Teddy Roosevelt wrote. Are there more?" Graham asked.

"Just Roosevelt and Kennedy. They're some of my most cherished books."

"Do you have a favorite? Are these all from your parents or what?"

"Yeah. Right over here, *Why England Slept*, it's the original manuscript. Jack Kennedy signed it for my father and sent it to him when he won his seat in Parliament. I don't know the whole story of how they met originally, but one time he mentioned a black-tie fundraiser that JFK's father was speaking at when he was the United States Ambassador to the United Kingdom. Even though my father was older than JFK, they apparently hit it off and kept in touch through the years. One time my father just about lost his mind over a missing wooden box of letters that apparently was correspondence between him and then-presidential candidate Kennedy. The box wasn't in the place he had left it, and he tore up his whole study searching for it. It turned out that the cleaning maids had moved the wooden box to the library, thinking my father brought it into his study from there. I never did figure out why it was such an ordeal, but it was probably the most visibly upset I had ever seen my father. That or the time I cracked a stained-glass window with a polo ball. But that's a story for another time. Anyways, as I said, I don't know how close my father was to JFK, but I do know that when Kennedy was president, he was planning on attending the opening of my parent's bookshop in Newport. All this to say, the *Why England Slept* manuscript is one of the few books that I can't imagine parting with. I inherited half these books from my parents or grandparents—the other half I've gotten on my own over the past 20 years. Since meeting Lucy, my purchases have slowed down some, but I still receive calls a few times a year from collectors all across the globe that reach out to me about rare books they think may be of interest to me."

"Pierce, I don't think I realized just how impressive your collection is. Your study alone has better pieces than any history museum I've seen. Albeit I haven't been to many."

"It would be hard to run a successful rare bookshop without any rare books, wouldn't it?"

"That's true. I just can't imagine you selling any of these."

"If I do need to sell them, I will. All I care about is that they fall into hands that deserve them. No matter how low the price point needs to be to make that happen."

"Do you have that new biography on Archie Neville in here?" Graham asked.

"Nope. That would be a waste of shelf space."

"Just thought that might bring in some special clients if you put that in the front window."

"That's not a bad idea. Let me make a few calls and see what I can get my hands on."

"Sounds good. Let me know what you hear back. When are the built-ins going in?"

"The carpenters are downstairs working on them now."

"Don't forget, I still need to talk to them about security measures. They know where the secret book case is going, correct? I need that to be perfectly aligned with where I'm putting in the vault door to the staircase. I will also need them to leave holes in the wooden framing for the security cameras."

"Yes, all of that was included in the contract."

"Did they ask any questions about it?"

"Not really, I just made it clear to them that I was storing the rarest books on the third floor, so we were going to be taking security very seriously. I think that seemed to make sense to them."

"Good, I will talk to the lead carpenter more tonight to make sure I can complete the work I need to complete. Now that they've arrived, we should get out of here and head to the Navy Yard. I think it's time we take a closer look around the USS *Constitution*. The director alerted the Secretary of the Navy this morning that we would be coming. So, we should have the ship to ourselves," Graham said.

"Did he give the secretary a reason for our visit?"

"I'm sure he came up with something clever, or maybe just said we were going to be on the ship, and no explanation was necessary. The director can be very persuasive."

"I've learned that the hard way more than a few times," I said as I nodded my head in agreement. Much like my father, the director usually got what he wanted. This was the case even before he ever obtained any impressive titles.

After touching base with the carpenters to confirm they had everything they needed to put in the new shelves, Graham and I started our walk to the Navy Yard. We took the same path that Lucy and I had. Graham took large steps compared to Lucy, so it was a fast walk. A lot less time spent smelling the roses or the hydrangeas in New England's case. We saw a few National Park Rangers in front of the nearby USS *Constitution* museum and approached them about touring the ship.

"FBI, we're here to take a look at the inside of the *Constitution*."

48

Graham had a few words with the park rangers. More often than not, the park rangers' role was to raise the flags, give the tours, and ensure that tourists didn't get lost. A visit from the FBI couldn't have been typical for their schedule.

"So, you are an adviser for the director of the FBI?" One of the park rangers inquired.

"Yes, I am."

"And what exactly do you advise on?"

"Well my education is in art history, but right now my focus is monuments in New England."

"I have worked for the National Park Service for two decades, and this is the first I am hearing about any *monument advisers* working for the FBI.

"It's a relatively new role."

"And what is it about the USS *Constitution* in particular that the FBI needs advising on?"

I shrugged my shoulders before responding.

"To be quite honest, they won't tell me. I'm just here to do my job."

"Seems tough to do your job without all of the information," the park ranger said skeptically.

"My thoughts exactly. Is it okay if I step on board now?"

"The sailors are aware of who you are, correct?"

"Yes."

"Then sure, go ahead," the park ranger said hesitantly as he pointed Graham and I towards the ship.

"What do you think, Pierce?" Graham asked as his black dress shoes squeaked across the ramp that guided us on board.

"I think it is good to be back on this ship again. I was too young to fully appreciate it last time I was on board."

"Who brought you last time?"

"My grandfather. It was kind of odd to tell you the truth. He spent the whole time below deck gliding his hand against the side of the ship. We spent almost an hour in this restricted area of the captain's cabin. But no one ever came to kick us out. My grandfather was just feeling the panels and drawing little sketches in his pocket notebook. I didn't

49

think too much of it at the time because he was constantly taking notes whenever we went to museums. But reflecting back on it now it was a little odd that we didn't explore the rest of the ship."

"What do you suppose he was sketching?"

"Just the cabin to my knowledge. My best guess is he wanted to better understand what his ancestors helped build, and since the cabin was a restricted area, he saw this as his best opportunity to do just that."

"Couldn't your grandfather have just said, "hey, my family helped build this ship and I would like to take a closer look at it." Seems like that would be an understandable request."

"Yeah, that wasn't his style. So, where do you want me?"

"Just look around as you please and see if you can come up with any reason why someone would want to steal this thing. My personal goal for today is just to find the best places to put our security cameras," Graham said.

"Okay, I can do that, just let me know if you need me. I may go check out that cabin. After revisiting that story about my grandfather I am kind of intrigued as to why he was so interested in it."

I went below deck and made my way to the captain's cabin. I walked around just like my grandfather had done, dragging my finger across every groove of the timber.

As I strolled around the inside of the cabin, I was asking myself one question.

What would drive someone to steal this piece of history?

If Archie Neville was recruiting Reaction Transport employees to join *The Response*—then there must be some pretty enticing incentives for those employees who are willing to partake in the company's side business.

"Alright, I think I am all set with the location for the cameras," Graham said as he loosened his tie and walked towards the staircase that would lead us back to the deck.

"Okay, is that all we needed to do for now?"

"Yeah, at least on my end. Did you find anything special about the cabin?"

"No, not really. It's interesting though, you can feel where the renovations have taken place."

"What do you mean?"

"I mean they have done a really good job with the renovations over the years. So good that if you were just looking at the ship you can hardly tell all the work that has been done."

"What's your point?"

"My point is when you drag your finger across this cabin you can feel the panels that have been replaced."

"And that means what?"

"I don't know if it means anything. It's just kind of funny to think that the ship has been around so long, and restored so many times, my ancestors probably wouldn't even recognize it on the inside. Take the captain's cabin for instance—I bet it looks totally different."

"Well, I'm sure the restorers did their best to stick to the original blueprints."

"Yeah, I suppose, but no matter how hard they tried, there's no way they could match it exactly to the original."

Graham shrugged his shoulders and began walking up the stairs.

I dragged my finger across one last panel before leaving. This panel in particular had definitely been replaced.

"Where to now, Graham?" I asked as I trailed behind him.

"Back to the bookshop to finish the installation of those cameras."

Upon our arrival back at the bookshop, I could see that the carpenters were still working on the bookshelves. So, to avoid disturbing their work, Graham and I went straight for the stairs and up to the study to have some dinner and discuss how Archie Neville and *The Response* could feasibly steal *Old Ironsides*.

"They can't sail it. I mean, technically, they can, but someone would notice before they finished the job. So, they'll need to find another way to move it. But how they do that, I have no idea," Graham said as he let out a sigh and threw his thick-lensed glasses across the table.

Graham dialed up his team of analysts to see if they had any updates on their end.

Meanwhile, I went down to check out the progress on the bookshelves. I was greatly impressed with the carpenters and their ability to carve the shelves into the exact framework I had envisioned for all of these years. The wood was a rich burgundy color; the top corners of the bookshelves were being carved into the shape of a lion's face, lion's faces with hollowed-out holes for eyes, to be exact. This is where Graham planned to place the security cameras. The feet of the shelves were elephants. Whose eyes would be fully intact.

"The shelves look amazing, gentlemen. I can't believe how quickly you've made this happen. I honestly can't thank you enough for your efforts."

"It's our pleasure, Mr. Spruce," the lead carpenter said as he continued to whittle away, "we should have it finished up after another 4-5 hours."

"That's wonderful," I said as I inspected one of the elephants, "so what time would you like to come back tomorrow?" I asked since it was already 5 p.m.

"If okay with you, we're thinking of finishing tonight since we already have our tools in the right place and are on a good roll," the carpenter answered.

"If you guys are up for it, that works for me. It would be great to have the shelves ready to start housing books by tomorrow morning. Just make sure you don't forget about the placement of the hidden vault as you finish the bookcase panel in front of it. I wouldn't want to wake up tomorrow and not be able to leave my house."

The carpenter nodded his head in agreement and kept on working.

At this rate, the bookshop could realistically open within the next few days.

Nine

"Wow, the place is really coming together," Graham said as he walked into the bookshop for the first time since the night prior when the carpenters were still finalizing the installation of the built-ins.

As promised, the carpenters were able to get the job done before midnight. I was so excited about the results that I couldn't bring myself to go to bed. I stayed up through the night until 4 a.m. to get the shop ready to go. I didn't think it was possible, but given the progress over the past 12 hours, I started to lean towards opening the shop up as soon as this afternoon.

"Yep. It took a few cups of coffee, but I'm feeling good about opening the place up after lunch today."

"Why would you have your grand opening in the middle of the same day you complete setting it up? You haven't even done any advertising yet. Didn't you go to business school? I figured they would've taught you the importance of marketing," Graham replied.

It was a valid question. I thought I learned a lot during business school, but I must've been daydreaming or working on my novel during my marketing course. I spent more time than I probably should've working on outlines for novels when I should've been studying. To be honest, I genuinely wouldn't care to explore most of the topics covered during graduate school on my own time, which is why I felt I needed the structure of University to learn it. Unlike art history, a subject I always thought I could get a Ph.D. on my own through books. I loved learning about art history as an undergrad. It was the subject I ended up majoring in. I was always thankful for how it shaped my world views, but no matter what you do, you have to understand business at the end of the day. That's what drove me to graduate school, not the aspiration to be a CEO, or an entrepreneur, merely the desire to better understand what individuals at that level understood. Graham was right that it was probably worth waiting to open the doors until after the papers did a feature on the shop. I still didn't plan to heed his advice, though. I was too excited to fulfill my parents' dream.

"Good point, Graham. I will consider that the next time I open a business. I thought you wanted to get moving so we could catch *The Response* faster?"

"Of course, that's what I want, but to make that happen, I also want this to come across as a legit business. You know—one that cares about its grand opening…"

"I do care about the grand opening. I care that it happens today."

"Hey, it's your bookshop, do as you please. Have you studied up on *The Response* profiles the analysts sent?"

"Yes I have. How did they get those anyway? The same way you got the financials?"

"No, we had one of the analysts apply for a job with Reaction Transport. But, unfortunately, he only made it about ten minutes before getting kicked out. Likely because we didn't have any military special operations experience on his resume—which we didn't realize at that point was a requirement to be considered for any position at Reaction Transport. But before he left the building, he managed to sneak into Toby Morgan's office and take a binder that read "BOSTON" on the spine. He must have said he needed to use the bathroom or something in order to sneak away. The "BOSTON" binder is what gave us more background on the six people we suspect are leading the mission to steal the USS *Constitution*."

"Your analysts really take a lot of risks to gather intelligence."

"You have no idea. So, *The Response* personnel folder. You have it memorized, right?"

"For the most part. They're all former military and currently work in the Operative Supply Chain Division at Reaction Transport."

"And you know what they look like?" Graham followed-up.

"Vaguely. Should books on Prime Ministers go in this section? Or would they look better over here next to the Presidents of the United States? Or over there above the shelf of European generals?"

"Pierce, you need to know their faces. Our whole plan relies on you being able to recognize these people if they come to the bookshop."

"I'm thinking right here next to the presidents."

"Pierce! If you mess this up, it won't matter where the books go. We have all the time in the world to worry about how you organize shelves, but if you want to open the bookshop up this afternoon, then I need to be confident that you know what you're doing."

Graham was right. I'm the first to admit that my mind was subject to wander when I had something that I viewed as important on it. I just wanted the shop to be in good shape. Rare book collectors know their stuff. I wanted them to view *Pierce's Rare Books on Bunker Hill* as a legitimate store, which in my mind, it was.

"Alright, let's go through the file again," I said.

"Here it is. Grab a cup of coffee and spend an hour with this. The director tells me you have a memory like a steel trap, so there should be no excuse for you not knowing everything the analysts back at the Bureau know about these people."

I've never been good at remembering faces. Unless that face is on a painting or a sculpture, then I am pretty good. As superior as my memory is when it comes to art, I spent so much time alone growing up that I was always far too overwhelmed when I was in groups to focus on one person's features or even their name. This further proved the kind of impact my early encounters with Archie Neville left because his face was oddly burned into my mind forever. I attributed my typical struggles to remember names and faces to a certain level of anxiety I've always had meeting new people. I recognize, just as people are so quick to point out in the tabloids, that I grew up with a silver spoon. Being mainly raised on an estate away from the common person made it much harder to relate. I do, of course, hope I've gotten better at this over the years. University and moving to London helped, but there were still times that I wish my parents would have let me interact with more children my age. Most of my exposure to other kids came during my visits to the United States. My grandparents were much more willing to take me into the local parks, where I would have a greater chance of encountering my peers. Anytime my parents took me places in London, it was most often for a fundraiser or private event to benefit my father. My parents were good people, but they often preferred to spend time alone with each other over bringing me along. So, when they did bring me—I was left to mingle amongst people that were over forty years my senior.

"Do you think one of them will show up today?" I asked.

"No, the papers don't even know you're here yet. My guess is by tomorrow, the Herald will figure it out, and by the following day, they'll have your bookshop on the front page of the paper. Then maybe we'll get some visitors."

"I guess I'm going to need the extra time anyway so I can do more research on *The Response*. But I'm not going to let the Herald or any other paper dictate when I open the doors," I said as Graham rolled his eyes in my direction.

"We got word that Archie Neville is in Vermont at the moment. It doesn't sound like he's up to much, more of a vacation."

"What part of Vermont is he in?"

"Stowe, have you ever been there?"

"Yeah, my grandparents used to ski up there. I went a couple of times but never cared for skiing much. The lodges in Vermont are some of the best places to read. I'm not surprised that's where he chose to go. Much easier to seclude himself there. It's pretty far away from the busier cities."

"Well, maybe after we deal with this mess in Boston—then we can go pay him a visit. I am relieved to have him located, though."

"Why do you think they only sent six *Response* members to Boston? I would think that stealing the *Constitution* would be a high enough level mission to require more of their resources? Even if they're highly trained, it's still a big ask," I said.

"It could be that they'll send more people to come the day of the heist. They tend to keep their people well spread out. I suppose to keep us guessing about where the next heist will happen."

"But you're 100% certain the USS *Constitution* is next on their list?"

"That is what the "BOSTON" binder that was taken from Toby Morgan's office indicated as the top priority, but who knows if that binder is current or accurate anymore," Graham answered.

"That's not reassuring."

"Might not be reassuring, but it's the best we can do at the moment. Don't forget that only a handful of people in the world outside of Reaction Transport employees know about *The Response*. We don't have enough bodies to stop all of the heists throughout New England. So we'll have to let some of the smaller ones go to prevent the large ones from happening. The smaller ones haven't garnered much attention from the media. But that's likely because they don't recognize that they're all connected. That's why we paused our search for the *Prescott* statue for a few days—no one believes it was stolen—they assume it's out for repairs. The news outlets haven't released anything indicating otherwise."

"Aside from the *Prescott* statue, have any other large monuments from Boston been taken?" I asked.

"Not that we know of, the *Prescott* statue was the first of its kind, other items consist mainly of art from various museums around the coast, and some volumes of old books from The Naval War College in Newport. But nothing else from Boston."

"How did they get those?"

"No idea. The Naval War College said there wasn't anything all that special about the books from their perspective. Just some old volumes on Civil War battles," Graham answered.

"Have the analysts found anything on where *The Response* is staying in Boston?"

"No, not yet. We have access to the records of all the hotels in the area but haven't found anything."

"If you were them, would you stay in a hotel?"

"Probably not—so it's just a matter of where they're hiding."

I wasn't pleased with where we stood at the moment. *The Response* held all the information we needed.

Who knows—the next heist could be happening right now.

That fact gave me chills.

Ten

Two weeks later

Waking up next to Lucy is something that I'll never take for granted. The first thing I typically do in the morning is pick up a paperback from my nightstand and start reading. But I don't think she realizes the amount of time I spend looking at her sleep each morning—even for just a few moments. Her lips always slightly pursed, curly dark auburn hair lying all over the pillow, arms stretched above her head, lifting her chest. As much as I enjoy reading about people who have been dead for decades—it's difficult some days to pull my eyes off of her.

"Good morning," I said. I could see her start to stretch a little.

"Were you watching me sleep?" She asked as she rolled over onto her side.

"Nope, I would never think of doing that. Do you want me to get up and make coffee?"

"Sure. I take it you didn't sleep well? You're in the same position you were in when I last saw you. You know, I don't think you have slept at all these past two weeks."

"It wasn't a great night. I guess I just have a lot on my mind. I've been able to get some good reading in because of it, though."

"What have you been thinking about?"

"I've just been thinking about how much our lives have changed since I opened the bookshop and whether I made the right decision doing it. I'm enjoying running the shop, but our progress on the actual operation has been non-existent so far. There's been no sign of any *Response* members. It makes me wonder if we need to be here. It could be that we made a huge mistake coming to Boston. I mean that I made a mistake in making us come. I fear that I took you from London when it wasn't necessary."

"We can always go back to London—don't worry about me. I'm enjoying Boston. No matter how long we end up staying."

"At this point, it might not be that much longer. If we don't hear anything in the next few weeks—then I think we should head back to England."

"Why would you say that? You just said that you enjoy running the bookshop?" Lucy reminded me.

"Yes. I do. But If I can't help the director with the real mission— then I have no idea what my purpose is here. Any assistance I have provided the director or Graham so far—I could've done via a few phone calls."

"You don't know that, Pierce. Maybe it will just take more time than you anticipated. But, you know as well as anyone you need to stay."

"I guess you're right, but it would be nice to see some progress soon."

Today was the 15th day that the shop was open, and thus far, it had been welcomed with excitement by Bostonians. We've stayed busy, and I've even sold a few dozen books. That part of our time in Boston has been encouraging. Although, I was a little worried that at some point people might figure out I'm practically giving away rare books. But for the time being I felt good about this business model.

"Here's your coffee, Pierce. Are you drinking it up here—or are you planning to go down to the shop?" Lucy asked.

I felt terrible that Lucy ended up making the coffee, considering I was the first one awake, and I originally made her the offer. But, honestly, I hadn't realized she left the bedroom. She must've snuck around me while I was thinking about what to do.

"Thank you for this," I said as I reached out my hand to grab the hot mug. "I'm going to head down to the shop early. We typically don't get our first customer until closer to 10 a.m., but I would like to get down there to make sure that everything is ready to go. I think I left some books out on the desks last night, so I should go pick those up. I need to get everything back in the right places. Someone wanted to buy my signed copy of Teddy Roosevelt's *The Naval War of 1812* yesterday, and it wasn't even supposed to be down there."

"How much did they offer you for it?"

"It wasn't so much about that—I just told them there was no way I could part with it. I need to move that one to the study before I forget. It was only down there because I was jotting down some notes about the war and the USS *Constitution*'s role in it."

"Has it been hard to part with the other books?" Lucy asked before taking a sip from her mug.

"Yeah. It's much more difficult than I anticipated. I knew how much the books meant to me going into it—or at least I thought I did. But I don't think I was ready for the emotional connection that breaks when you sell a book. The only thing that makes it tolerable is knowing that someone else might enjoy the book as much as I have and hopefully pass it down to the next generation."

That is what my parents had always wanted—but it wasn't until now that I felt I was ready to grant my parents' wish.

"I'm sure they will, Pierce. You have plenty of books. No need to be selfish and keep them all for yourself."

I took a sip from my mug.

"No response?" Lucy said as her brows raised.

"No. No. You're right."

She smiled and left me for the shower.

It was around 7:30 a.m. I usually head to the study before going downstairs to the shop, but I felt like I needed to get to work. Graham had mainly been staying out of the bookshop so as not to be seen. Most days, he usually came down before I opened the doors—then we did lunch in the study together at Noon. Then, at night—he comes back down again to help me lock up.

We put display screens in the study for Graham to keep an eye on things from above and so he can tell if any *Response* members enter. With cameras secretly embedded by Graham in the eyes of two of the lions carved into the built-in shelves, he could get a view of the entire bookshop. The security cameras have made no difference so far. Most of our guests have been tourists who've read about the bookshop in the papers. People have come from all over to see the books, and I guess to meet me. Ever since the Herald ran a piece on me soon after the bookshop opened, we were getting a few dozen people coming through each day just to get a picture with me—which to me, seemed like a complete waste of their time. Either come for the books or don't come at all. It frustrated me that my presence in the shop seemed to be a distraction from the books. I didn't open the bookshop to bring more attention to myself, but given the media exposure, I'm sure it's difficult for locals to believe that.

I finally rolled out of bed, showered quickly, and took my coffee downstairs.

I spent about 30 minutes cleaning things up and preparing to open the doors. It was close to 9:00 a.m. I went ahead and unlocked the doors a few minutes early—taking my post behind the large desk in front of the wall to wall built-ins. The lions that the carpenters so skillfully carved stared down on me from the upper corners of the high ceiling. Graham was stationed at his usual post, up in the study in front of the screens. I pulled a book off the shelves to keep me occupied while waiting for the first visitors to arrive.

For today I chose a first edition of *The Great Gatsby* by F. Scott Fitzgerald. I read *Gatsby* at least once a year. Every time I read that book, I think about what it would be like to be someone else—someone new. I struggle every day with my fears of being Pierce Spruce. The person in charge of carrying on a family dynasty. A dynasty I never asked for and wasn't sure how to go about keeping it alive. I couldn't help but feel anxiety every time I thought about it. I was certainly feeling it now when I considered the challenges Graham and I faced. Despite Lucy's encouragement this morning. I was still asking myself the question—do I have what it takes?

Others in the world probably thought my life had no challenges. But, unfortunately, I knew far too well that was false. I have many challenges and doubts about my abilities to conquer them—just like anyone, I assume.

I was just a few pages into *Gatsby* when my first customer walked through the door. Things had picked up the past few days in terms of activity in the shop. There could be 3-5 visitors at any given time, either just passing by or taking advantage of one of the desks to check out some of the books. For now there was just one—a young boy—no older than twelve.

"Excuse me, would you like any help?" I asked the boy who was eyeing the fiction shelves.

"Yes, can you get me that one over there, please? I know that is the one I want," he quickly responded while pointing out the spine he wanted me to grab for him.

This took me off guard. The boy seemed to know exactly what he was after.

"How do you know this is the book you want? Have you seen it before?" I asked, a bit surprised by the selection.

He paused for a moment before responding. He'd already begun setting his eyes on the first chapter.

"I guess I don't know for sure, but I'm assuming I'll like it because I've liked the other two books I've read by this author," he replied.

I was impressed, especially by someone so young.

"Well, it's a good choice. May I ask what your name is?"

"Patrick."

"Nice to meet you, Patrick. My name is Pierce."

"Hi Pierce—I'm really glad you opened this bookstore."

"Patrick, kids like you are one of the many reasons I did so."

"Really?! What are the other reasons?"

"Those are a secret—just know you made my day today. So, you've read other books by Fitzgerald?"

"Of course, haven't you? If you haven't, then I should leave this book on the shelf so you can read it yourself."

I chuckled, "I have indeed, in fact I was reading him right before you came through that door. But I'm more fascinated by the fact that you have."

"Why is that fascinating?"

When I thought about that statement, I realized that there are still children out there that love books as much as I did at that age.

"I guess it shouldn't be. Are there any others that you would like? I have plenty more Fitzgerald novels and short stories in my study that I would be happy to bring down for you to look at."

"No, not today. I would love to see them sometime, but I have to go home, and I only have enough allowance for one book this month. How much does this one cost?" Patrick asked.

"Well, how much do you have?"

"This is all. If I need to come back next month with more I would understand. I'm visiting my dad this weekend and I wanted something to read during the car ride," he said as he handed me a five-dollar bill.

"Where does your dad live?"

"Maine. He and my mom are divorced, so I spend a lot of time in the car going back and forth."

My head dropped when the boy confirmed my assumption.

"Let's say the book is $5 and call it a deal."

"Deal. It's been a pleasure doing business with you," Patrick said as he reached out his hand.

I returned the handshake and wrapped up the book for him in some fancy paper.

That first edition Fitzgerald was in the best hands it could possibly be in, and for five bucks, I would say that he got a pretty good deal, but honestly, it was me that got the better end of it. This was exactly the kind of transaction my parents dreamed of when they first thought up the idea of starting a rare bookshop.

A few hours went by with more and more customers coming through, but none as special as the first. By 11:30 a.m. there were so many people in the shop asking questions—I couldn't continue my reading of *Gatsby* at all. I was just about to flip the "open" sign to "closed" for the lunch hour when a customer came through the door that I felt like I recognized from somewhere. The trouble was, I couldn't tell if I knew him from coming into the shop on another day or if I recognized him from *The Response* file. I thought that maybe if I talked to him, I could get a better look at his face.

"Can I help you find a book?" I asked.

"Just looking around. Heard there was a new bookstore in town and figured I needed to see what all of the fuss was about," the customer answered.

I was 95% sure that this was a member of *The Response*, based on some of the photos the analysts sent along with the profiles, but it was hard to know for certain until I could get more information.

"Well, let me know if you need anything, and I would be happy to help. Are you from around here?"

"No, I'm from Canada. I moved here for my graduate program."

"Good for you. What're you studying?"

"Art history."

"What kind of art? I was an art history major myself."

"18th - 19th Century paintings mostly. My goal is to work at the Smithsonian."

"That's interesting. To be honest, I don't meet many other art history majors. I'm glad to hear there are still others interested in the topic. Do you enjoy rare books as well?"

"Yes. I do. I see you have a copy of *Why England Slept* on your desk. Anything special about that one?" He asked.

At this moment, I realized I still hadn't brought those personal books back up to the study like I told Lucy I would.

"President Kennedy signed it and gave it to my father. They had met when they were young and kept in touch through the years. When my father won his seat in Parliament—he received this professionally bound manuscript for the book—with a nice note inside congratulating him on his achievement, and opportunity to serve the people of Buckinghamshire."

"What a story. Can I see it?"

I wasn't sure if I should trust him. I had a gut feeling he was one of the men we were after, but I also didn't want to blow my cover. I felt like I had to let him see the book.

"Sure. You can open it up on my desk. I typically don't let people look at that one since it's a family heirloom, but I can make an exception for a fellow art historian."

"How come it's out? Is someone trying to buy it?"

"No. I would never sell it. It's usually up in my study, but I pulled it out and brought it down here last night. I read it from time to time when I'm thinking about my father."

I was already saying too much, but I didn't know what else to do. I wanted to keep the conversation going for as long as possible. At least until I was able to figure out where *The Response* was staying. Along with the security cameras, Graham also had audio set up to listen in if a situation like this arose. I wanted to allow him to hear the potential *Response* member talk as much as possible in the case he may share anything useful. Even if it wasn't the information we truly wanted—their location.

"I can't believe he signed this, and you weren't kidding about the personal note," the customer said.

"You thought it wasn't in there?"

"I just thought it was a copy of his signature or something. Some kind of signed copy that people who donated a lot of money to his campaign would've received."

"No. It's the real deal. I should probably put that on the shelf over here, so I don't leave it out again."

I was trying to be patient, but I wanted to get my father's book out of his hands.

"Anything else you would like to take a look at?" I said as I snatched the bound manuscript.

"Not right now. I should probably get going. I have a class this afternoon and have already been late once this week," he said before making a move for the door.

I let out a sigh of relief when he walked out the door. Honestly,

I doubted anyone had ever held the JFK manuscript that wasn't me, my father, my grandfathers, or Jack Kennedy. I shouldn't have let him pick it up in the first place, but it was partially my careless mistake for leaving it out.

It was a strange encounter.

My palms were clammy at this point. I needed to empty the shop so I could debrief with Graham. I scurried around the shop—trying to clear the place out without being rude to my real customers. Finally, once the last person walked out the door, I was able to flip the sign.

Closed.

I opened up the security vault Graham had put in behind the hidden bookcase door. Once through, I sprinted upstairs to the study.

"That was one of them! Alexander Andrews," Graham shouted and threw down his headphones as I came through the door. I was still in shock. He seemed to be elated.

"That was Andrews? Do we know for sure?" I asked.

"That was definitely him."

"I'm sorry I couldn't get more information out of him. It didn't go how I expected it would."

"Pierce, for your first time being "undercover," it went pretty well. These things never go quite as planned. It was far-fetched to think we could get one of them to give away where they are staying to begin with. If it were that easy—I wouldn't have a job."

"I suppose. Were you able to get any helpful information from our conversation?"

"Well, for one, even if we don't know the exact place they're staying, we know that they're in Boston and can safely assume that there are more *Response* members here with Andrews."

"Do you still think they're staying in Charlestown?" I asked.

"I'm not sure, but I'm more confident now, having seen one of them. I need to go back to the *Constitution* tonight. I'll get a few more cameras to set up to ensure that we have the entire perimeter of the ship covered. We shouldn't tell anyone this time. I'll plan to head over there alone. I need to be as stealthy as possible. No one can know about these cameras. They'll be an additional live stream through our monitors here," Graham said.

"If it's best for you to go alone, then I'll stick around here. Anything I can do while I'm home tonight?"

"Not that I can think of at the moment. Why don't you plan to let me take the work for tonight. You feel free to spend some time with Lucy. I know you've been working around the clock in the bookshop for the past few weeks. You should enjoy a night with your wife."

"If you say so, Graham. Just let me know if you change your mind. I may head back downstairs to open things back up. What time are you thinking about heading out?"

If I couldn't go with Graham back to the *Constitution*—opening the bookshop for the remainder of the day seemed like the most helpful thing I could do.

"Yes, please do. We don't want anyone to think anything strange is going on. I will most likely leave a little later this afternoon. There is an FBI Field Office a few miles away. I need to get some equipment from there first. Then I'll head to the *Constitution* later on tonight. It should only take an hour or so to set up the additional cameras."

"Alright, let's plan to have a drink tonight in the study. I'll have them ready for when you get back so we can debrief."

"Sounds good, but you may as well stop making me drinks. You know I'll never have one while on duty," Graham confirmed.

"Fine. But one of these days when you're "off duty," if that ever happens, then you'll need to let me fix you up an old fashioned."

"Whatever you say, Pierce."

I left the study and went back downstairs to the shop.

I flipped the sign in the window.

Open.

Eleven

The afternoon was relatively slow. Few people even wanted to check out any books. They just strolled in, made a loop around the shop, and left. They must've been tourists, but I still wish they would've shown a little more interest in the books. On a positive note, the slow afternoon did give me time to finish my reading of *Gatsby* and tidy up a few shelves. The shop was starting to come together. I checked my watch. It was a few minutes past five and time to close up. I check my watch frequently. I'm not sure why. It's not like time moves faster or slower than I think it does. You would assume that after 41 years, I would break this habit. My father gave me this Cartier tank on my 21st birthday, which could be the real reason why I like to look at it so much, especially during difficult times.

CRASH!

My head perked up from my watch.

I went to look outside to see what caused the loud noise. As soon as I swung the door open to inspect the commotion—I felt someone's forearm swing across my throat and wrap tightly around my neck. My head began to twist at what felt like 180 degrees. I thought for sure it was about to pop off of my shoulders. A hand was cupped over my mouth and nose—making it impossible to breathe. My legs began to flail, time now felt like it was passing slowly, but of course, I could not look at my watch to confirm. My lungs ballooned with air that I couldn't let out. The blood flowing through my body now seemed to be shooting to everywhere except my head and staying there. Right, when I thought it all was going to end—I was thrown into the bricks below the bookshop's front windows. My back slammed against the front side of the bookshop and my body folded to the ground. While I was lying on the concrete—I could see a man—though my vision was blurry. The man was walking out of the shop with a book in his hand.

"Thank you for the gift, Mr. Spruce. Admiral Neville will be pleased to add this to his bookshelf—or maybe just use it to start a fire."

I tried to get a good look at the man, but all I could see was the *Why England Slept* manuscript.

The next thing I saw was the side of a boot closing in on my face.

CRACK!

It connected with my jaw, and everything went dark.

Twelve

My head was pounding. It was difficult to open my eyes because of the swelling. I've never experienced pain like this in my life. As I attempted to stare at the ceiling, trying to figure out what happened to me, it crossed my mind that this was my first experience getting hit.

I could faintly hear footsteps coming up the stairs. Hopefully, it was Lucy with a bag of ice and a cocktail.

"How are you doing, Pierce?"

It was Graham. How was he here right now? He was supposed to be putting the extra cameras in around the *Constitution*.

"Been better," I answered.

"I bet. Do you like working for the FBI yet?"

Graham set an old fashioned on my chest. I would probably need a straw to drink it.

"I don't work for the FBI. I work for *Pierce's Rare Books on Bunker Hill*, and we just got robbed."

"Were you able to get a look at either of the perps?"

"Not a good one. There was a loud noise that sounded like someone

David Lowe Cozad

threw a metal trash can down the street. That's what caused me to open the door and see what was going on. The next thing I knew, my head was getting twisted like a bottle cap, and I couldn't breathe—then I was slammed down against the bricks. I caught sight of one man who came out of the shop with a book but couldn't identify which *Response* member it was. I couldn't make out which book it was either until he came in front of me and said he was taking the book back to Archie Neville as a souvenir. It was the *Why England Slept* manuscript. That was the last I saw of him. The next thing I knew, his goon kicked me in the face."

"I'm sorry I wasn't around to protect you, Pierce. I shouldn't have left you alone. This will never happen again. I promise you that," Graham said with a slight quiver in his voice.

I don't know how Graham could make such a promise or why he was apologizing. It wasn't totally his fault that this happened. I should've known something like this was coming. It was only a matter of time before Archie Neville figured out what I was really doing in Boston.

"None of this is your fault, Graham."

"Yes, it is. I promise you that for the remainder of this operation, I won't leave your side. That is, if you're still up for sticking around—the director and I need you."

I mustered up all the energy I could to lift the highball glass off of my chest. Finally, I was able to get a small sip of whiskey and didn't even need a straw, although the numbness on the side of my mouth made it difficult, so some of the cocktail trickled down my chin. The warmth from the whiskey that did make its way down my throat soothed some of my pain. Graham didn't know me well enough yet to know that what happened tonight only motivated me to stay and help that much more. Before today I was still on the fence about my purpose in Boston. Now, I knew I couldn't leave. The JFK manuscript was one of the few pieces of my father I had left, and *The Response* ripped it from me. The heist was personal. Something had to be done about it.

"I'm not going anywhere. You better make sure I don't get my head kicked in again, though. I'm only as good as my brain, one more of those kicks to the head, and I will be completely worthless."

72

"You'll shake it off. It gets better after a few days, I swear. Take it from someone that gets hit in the head all the time," Graham said in an attempt to comfort me.

"I always wondered why you act the way you do."

It hurt to laugh, but it felt good to know that my wit was still intact, even if my jaw wasn't.

"So, they have the JFK manuscript? I thought that was in the study?" Graham asked.

"I meant to bring it back upstairs earlier this morning after that *Response* member showed up. I somehow forgot to grab it when I ran up at lunch to talk to you. I just wasn't thinking the shop would get robbed."

"Pierce. You have millions of dollars in value of books sitting on a wall for everyone to see. It never crossed your mind that the shop could get robbed? By *The Response* or otherwise?"

"No, not really, to be honest. I figured the extra security measures were more so to keep us safe—not the books."

"You view the world through rose-colored glasses, Pierce. It might just get you killed."

"Did you get the cameras put in place?" I asked.

"Yes, I got them put into place. Speaking of cameras—I was just about to pull up the video footage from earlier tonight. Maybe we can get a visual on who beat you up," Graham said.

There were more exciting things in the world to watch than replays of your head getting stomped, but I guess it was necessary.

"I can't see at the moment but go ahead and pull it up," I told Graham.

We sat there for 30 minutes or so. Graham ran and re-ran the video. He didn't say much, but I could imagine the gears turning in his head. He finally spoke up.

"Well, the man who stole the manuscript is almost certainly not the man who was in the shop earlier. He is much shorter—it appears to be Toby Morgan based on his size. I have some bad news, though."

"What's that?"

"The person who strangled you. He's about 6'7 and somewhere

around 300 pounds. No one in our records fits that description, meaning that there are more than the six *Response* members here in Boston."

Weirdly it made me feel better that the man who beat me up was such a giant. I have a reasonably sized frame, but only to do certain things like play polo. The only thing I needed my body to do athletically, at least that was the case before working with Graham. My 6 foot tall, 170-pound build makes it much easier to run away from someone that size than it does to fight.

"I'll send these recordings to the analysts in Washington to see if they can identify the hulk here."

I heard footsteps on the stairs again. Thank goodness Lucy was coming up to the study. She'll be a much more comforting presence than Graham.

"How is the patient?" She asked as she took a seat next to me on the chesterfield sofa.

"Been better," I said as I rested my head back on the couch and laid an ice pack back over my eyes.

Lucy stayed with us and chatted for a while. The conversation was easy, and we learned a lot about our new friend Graham. It turns out that he grew up in a lower-middle-class apartment complex in Brooklyn, New York. Which I guess he mentioned to me in London when talking about that old baseball player. He's an only child, just like I am, but we grew up on opposite sides of the wealth spectrum. Graham's mother worked very hard to provide him with everything he needed to have the opportunity to succeed in life. It turns out he had never left New York City until he enlisted in the Marines, and they sent him to Vietnam soon after graduating high school. He didn't speak about the war, but I hoped he would tell me more about it someday over a drink.

Since I grew up so isolated, I never got to know anyone my age on a personal level—certainly never had a close friend. I left the topic alone and didn't pry anymore. It felt good to relax and have someone to talk to—I didn't want to ruin it because of my curiosity.

I took the final sip of my old fashioned. My eyelids were heavy from the swelling, and I needed some rest.

Everything went dark again.

Thirteen

One week later

It took a week, but I was finally turning a corner, only occasionally having migraines throughout the day that felt like pins were pressing into my head from all directions. This is no surprise, given the trauma I endured. I just prayed that the pain would cease soon. Along with the end of the countless headaches, I was looking forward to waking up in the morning and not seeing the same black eye and a bruised jaw. But I guess I was thankful I could see at all. All things considered, I was confident that the incident with *The Response* wasn't going to impact me long term except for the stolen JFK manuscript. Having that stolen was what was keeping me up at night more so than any physical ailment.

Things have been relatively calm since the shop has been closed. I tried to open it a few hours at a time just so my new clients didn't think anything strange was happening. We were monitoring the cameras surrounding the *Constitution* and the shop with no success. There was no sight of *The Response* since my beating. I must say I'm still embarrassed. I feel like a fool, not just that I got tricked by *The Response* during what would be my first real test, but also the fact that I had no prayer of defending myself. Graham tried to console me, indicating that any coward who surprises someone from behind and chokes them out can win a fight, but I was still fearful that even if *The Response* had attacked me head-on, I would have been a sitting duck. Growing up, I was much more comfortable reading books than I ever was roughhousing. My father was the only person around that might have been able to educate me in that regard. I assumed he must have learned some self-defense techniques in his Royal Navy training, but he was never around long enough to spend time with me on those sorts of things.

In moments of fear, I had to remind myself of what I could control, the things I did know, and how I might be able to help Graham. If I couldn't take down *The Response* with my physicality, then I needed to do everything in my power to take them down with my mind.

In the study, I laid out a few books I had on the War of 1812, including the first edition work by Teddy Roosevelt and books on the geography of New England. I tried to see what I could find out about the USS *Constitution* and its role in Charlestown. Understanding the Charlestown landscape became essential as we searched for the thieves.

I kept my nose in the books for the next six hours or so. Lucy came up a few times to check on me, but I think she got the hint that I needed to focus on my work. It took everything in me not to shut my eyes and take breaks every fifteen minutes or so, which must have been a bi-product of the head trauma. Lucy was concerned that I was already exerting my brain too much after the damage to my head, but I didn't feel like there was any other option.

I kept reading.

The USS *Constitution*'s nickname "*Old Ironsides*" came during the War of 1812. This was when the ship was in its prime, and cannonballs simply bounced off her hull. *Old Ironsides* wasn't just successful in battle; she was also used as a training vessel during the Civil War and even transported art to France at one point. That's a fact I did know previously, presumably from one of my art history courses or something like that.

I wasn't sure what any of this meant to *The Response.* My gut told me not much of anything. I recognized that Neville's ancestors fought in both the Revolutionary War and the War of 1812, but why was the USS *Constitution* so important to him? Surely those familial ties alone weren't the only driving force he had to pursue stealing the ship now, over a century and a half later. Revenge for his ancestors couldn't be the only thing on his mind—there had to be more to it than that. It wasn't like stealing smaller items such as artwork or the JFK manuscript. So, why attempt such a difficult heist? And why would he put his whole company at risk to do it? They can't turn around and sell it—although I was curious how much it would be worth.

"Studying up?" Graham asked as he entered the room. As always, he was in full suit and tie and appeared ready to work.

"Just trying to see if history can point us in the right direction," I answered.

"How's that going for you?" Graham asked as he grabbed a seat next to me on the sofa.

"It's going okay, unfortunately, no book explains why these scumbags want to steal the *Constitution.*"

"Pierce, if you're trying to figure out why *The Response* is doing all of this, then you might as well not waste your time with old history books."

I didn't want to admit it, but Graham had a point.

"I don't know where else to turn though, Graham. *The Response* seems to be able to do whatever they want."

"If they can do whatever they want, then why do you think they have chosen to focus on the *Constitution?* It's not like they can do anything with it."

"Well, they can't make any money off of it. At least not by selling it. And if people knew they were responsible for stealing it, then they would have no way of continuing their other businesses. They would have too big of a target on their back."

This theory made sense to me, but it was unclear if Graham felt the same way.

"Exactly. Pierce, the reason why *The Response* is so dangerous is that we have no idea as to "why" they're doing what they're doing."

"Have you ever seen anything like this in your time working at the Bureau, Graham? An enemy with unknown motives—seemingly willing to risk their livelihood over what would appear to be mostly symbolic items?"

"You hear stories at Quantico and read case studies where the enemy has no desire for recognition or notoriety. Of course, groups like this are the most dangerous, but usually, they at least have a clear motive," Graham said.

We may not know "why" Archie Neville started *The Response*. But we knew they were a competent, well-resourced enemy.

Those facts alone meant we were fighting an uphill battle.

Fourteen

"How are you feeling?" Lucy asked.

She had made her way back up to the study to check on me once again. She remained concerned that I was overdoing things so soon after my injuries.

"Not bad, about 80%," I answered.

"I will take Pierce Spruce at 80% over anyone else I know at 100, but you better be telling me the truth because if you're lying, I may be the next person coming after you."

"Then you must not know a lot of people," I tried to keep the conversation light-hearted so she wouldn't continue to worry about me.

"Has Graham figured out who did this to you?"

"He was just in here about an hour ago. We know who did it. We just don't know where they are."

Ring...Ring...

Lucy went over to the other side of the study to answer the phone.

"Spruce residence. This is Lucy."

"Hi Lucy, this is the director. I'm looking for Pierce."

"Hi Mr. Director, yes, he's right here."

I grabbed the phone from Lucy with a little bit of hesitation. I hope the director wasn't disappointed with my performance. Hopefully, my getting jumped didn't compromise our mission to the point of no return.

"Mr. Director," I said into the phone.

"How are you feeling, Pierce? I tried to call you a few times this past week to check on you, but then I thought it was better to bother Agent Graham for updates so you could rest," the director said.

"Lucy figured it was you and that you wouldn't be offended. We unplugged the phone for a while because hearing that ring was painful."

"That's what Graham said. I saw the tape. You must have a strong chin because a lot of people would still be lying on the ground after that."

"If I were anything like my father—I would have done a lot more than just survive."

"Why is that thought even crossing your mind, Pierce? Listen, in this line of work, you can't do that. You can't let yourself overthink a situation that you have no control over, and you certainly can't compare how you handled something to how anyone else may have handled it."

The director knew as well as anyone what I meant. My father, and others like him, people like Special Agent Graham, and the director himself, would've been able to handle that situation without giving up the manuscript.

"You know, Mr. Director, in the just over three weeks since I've been here, we've made little progress. Do you think this was the wrong move on both of our parts? Before the attack, I was 50/50 whether I should stay or go."

"The key to that statement is that you were 50/50 before the attack, which means that even with those thoughts going through your head, you still opened up the bookshop and kept at it. And you're still here now—I don't think you're considering leaving. So why don't you cut the crap, Pierce, and start doing what I brought you here to do? Which is not to fight; it's to tap into that wealth of knowledge you're hiding."

"And how would you like me to do that, Mr. Director? How can I help Graham?"

"Tell me how you would steal the USS *Constitution*? Tell me where you would keep the stolen statue of *Colonel Prescott*? You know Archie Neville well enough. I want you to put yourself in Archie Neville's shoes and tell me what you would do to pull this off," he said.

"I don't know. Graham and I agree that we wouldn't try to sail the *Constitution*."

"Why?"

"Too big, too slow, been too many years since its glory days."

"How would you take it if it can't sail fast enough?"

"It would need to be assisted in moving. Pushed, pulled, lifted, I don't know how, but there's no other way to get it out of the Navy Yard."

"Good, now you're getting the hang of it. So, where would you take it?"

"I don't know—maybe France."

"Why in the world would you go to France?"

"In the late 1870s, the *Constitution* transported a shipload of American art for an exposition in Paris. Of course, there's no way they could get it there without getting caught by the Coast Guard, but that's what I would do. Load the cargo hold up with the other artifacts they have stolen, and head off to Europe. It would be symbolic, I guess."

"Let's say you were going to bring it to Paris. How?"

"You couldn't—not without being seen."

"Not good enough! How would you do it if you had to?"

"I would pull it with a ship that was capable of towing it."

"Interesting. You see, Pierce, in just a few minutes, you've already provided more value to me than many of my agents. My agents would have just told me the outcome that was 99% likely given their training. On the other hand, you just gave me the other 1% by suggesting they would try and tow the ship to Paris. You can think outside the box in a way that's far rarer than you could ever imagine. That's a valuable trait, and if you keep at it, and keep vocalizing your thought process, then that thinking will help Agent Graham crack this case. That 1% thought process is exactly why you're the man for the job. The only man for the job," the director said.

"Thank you, Mr. Director. I needed this phone call."

"I am glad it was helpful and that you're starting to feel a little better. Take care of yourself, Pierce. We will talk again soon."

The director hung up the phone before I could speak any further. I wanted to keep talking and make sure that we would not ease up on *The Response* even when we find the *Prescott* statue and prevent the heist of the USS *Constitution*. I wanted confirmation that we wouldn't stop until I got the *Why England Slept* manuscript back.

He was gone before I could confirm. He's a busy man. To think that dealing with *The Response* is just a fraction of his daily workload amazed me. Maybe I should have been cutting him a little more slack these past few years.

Fifteen

I put my watch back on. I'd been fiddling with it in my hands while I was on the phone with the director. I grabbed a few of the books I had been studying and went to meet with Graham who was waiting for me on the second floor. I also brought some research materials that I recently acquired on Colonel William Prescott. Before today we hadn't focused our attention as much as I thought we should be on recovering the statue. The missing statue may have been what tipped off *The Response*'s presence in Boston to the analysts, but it was the assumption that the USS *Constitution* was next on the list that was driving our decision-making, and therefore our focus. This may have been a mistake on our part. Instead of focusing solely on preventing the heist of the *Constitution*, I thought it might do Graham and I some good to spend more time searching for the items that were already missing. Particularly the statue of *Colonel Prescott*.

"How's it going, Graham?" I asked as I laid my research across the coffee table in the living room.

"Going good. How are you?"

"Not bad. I think I'm slowly getting my ability to read and focus back. I was just on the phone with the director, and he shared some thoughts that woke me up a bit."

"That's good to hear. Sometimes we all need that extra push when we're down. Do the two of you talk on the phone often?"

"I think we have talked more the past few weeks than we have in the past five years combined."

"It surprises me that the two of you aren't closer. I mean, if he's your godfather, he must have been around some when you were young. He obviously trusts you quite a bit to bring you in on this mission."

"Yes, we were very close when I was younger. But things changed, and we had some disagreements through the years."

I left it at that. Just like Graham wasn't ready to share any more details about his experiences in Vietnam, I also wasn't prepared to explain my falling out with the director to him. Not at this time, at least.

"Understood," Graham said, making it clear he had no interest in prying into my personal business with the director, just so long as it didn't negatively impact our operation.

"Graham, I think it would do us some good to switch gears for a little—to focus on recovering the *Prescott* statue instead of solely thinking about protecting the *Constitution*."

"Why do you say that? Our working assumption is that the statue is well on its way to Vermont with all of the other artifacts. The statue is less valuable to us than the *Constitution* is. Plus, once we catch *The Response* mid heist, we can tie them back to Neville and go search the cabin at that time."

"I understand that line of thinking, but you and I both know that we need a win. Maybe *The Response* needs to know that someone cares about these monuments enough to risk getting in their way."

"I think I could get on board with that approach, just as long as we don't forget that we are still responsible for ensuring nothing happens to the *Constitution*. The president doesn't have to give an address to anyone about a missing statue, but if the *Constitution* disappears—people will demand answers. The director made it clear that the last thing he, or the president, needs right now is more bad press. The budget cuts alone have garnered enough publicity for a while," Graham responded.

"Of course, Graham. So, here's what I'm thinking," I said as I sprawled out even more notes and maps of New England across the tabletop. Graham and I spent the rest of the day and night researching everything we had in our possession about the statue and Colonel Prescott's efforts during the Revolution. Hoping some piece of this knowledge may help us better understand why *The Response* chose this statue in particular.

We enjoyed ourselves, and Graham seemed to be getting more comfortable working with a novice in most of the skills needed to be competent in his profession. However, I did get the feeling that my own strengths as a researcher were beginning to warm him up to the idea that I could actually add some value to the operation. Maybe it took me getting beat up for both of us to loosen up a little bit. So much so that I almost convinced him to have a cocktail. That is where he drew the line, though. Knowing that the mission wasn't going to go how we drew it up forced us to improvise and seek new outside-of-the-box strategies.

We moved back up to the study after dinner and stayed up late looking through books, maps, notes, and everything the analysts had on file about the *Prescott* heist. We were making significant progress. At least it felt like progress. By the time 1:00 a.m. rolled around, we decided to call it a night and agreed we would sleep in the next day.

My alarm went off at 8:00 a.m. the following morning. It was the first time I planned to open up the bookshop for a full day of service since I was beat up. The Boston summer was continuing to require me to wear short-sleeved button-up shirts and shorts to stay cool in the shop. I still hadn't figured out what bookshop owners should wear to work, but I suppose it was safe to say that I was consistently underdressed compared to what my father used to wear to work at the bank and Parliament. Good thing I was my own boss, I guess. I slipped on my black Crockett & Jones loafers with the tassels and headed to the living room. Of course, I walked in, and Graham was in a suit and tie like he always was. I suppose I was consistently underdressed compared to him too.

"Morning, Graham. I would offer you food, but I see you already helped yourself. How'd you sleep?"

"I slept pretty well actually. The director called us again this morning to see how last night went. I told him that we wanted to spend some more time tracking down the *Prescott* statue. I explained to him how we think it may help lead us to *The Response*'s location—which will then lead us to their plans regarding the *Constitution*." Graham chewed as he spoke.

"What did the director have to say about that plan?" I said as I finally grabbed a scone for myself and started to gnaw at it.

"He thinks it's a good idea as well," Graham confirmed.

"Did he have any new insights for us?" I asked as I took another bite.

"If he had new insights, wouldn't he go to you first? You're his favorite, after all. He's still mad at me for allowing *The Response* to beat you up," Graham said as he gave me a shrug of his shoulders.

If I had decided to tell Graham all the details about just how strained my relationship with the director had been during the years since he took on his current role, and why we no longer talked until now—he would know I wasn't the favorite.

"I don't know about that. What I do know is that we need to get on the offensive. As we discussed last night, if we can get the statue back, it will more than likely lead to more information about *The Response*'s next moves."

Graham took a sip of coffee. I readied myself for his feedback; it was easy to tell he was mulling over what I just said. As of last night, he was on board for shifting our focus to the *Prescott statue*, but since we had such limited resources, I wasn't sure if his mind would cool on that plan after sleeping on it. He put his mug down. I heard the seeping hot coffee shoot down his throat. Then he spoke up.

"You think they might sink it?" Graham asked.

"The statue? Yeah, I do. The director doesn't think they'll destroy anything. He keeps reiterating that to us, but I don't see any proof that they're above such acts. Their moral compass doesn't appear to be functioning at a high level. I agree it's not their first choice, but if they know we're after them, after the statue, they might just destroy it and move on. That's how I feel, at least. They would rather see it destroyed than risk being caught."

"Where does that leave us?" Graham asked.

"It leaves us with the fact that they know what they're doing, and their plan is thoughtful. It means that we need to stop thinking about what they might do and act on what they've done. We need to continue to keep working like that, putting our heads together and trying to get ahead of them, at least by a few moves."

"I agree—I hadn't thought about it in those terms, but you're right."

"Here's what I think we should do. First, we will need to reach out to the Coast Guard."

"Pierce, we can't do that."

"I still don't fully understand why not? Even if we don't mention *The Response* at all?"

"We can't ask for help from anyone. You know the president's take on this—no more government resources."

"So, we'll never have any additional help? Even if the USS *Constitution* gets taken?"

"None. That's why you're the one paying for everything at the moment. That's why the top-secret FBI records show Pierce Spruce, New England Monument Adviser (Volunteer) as the sole owner of this operation."

"Volunteer? The FBI came to me about all of this."

"No one can ever know the FBI has anything to do with this. It has to seem like you did this by your choosing."

"Is there anything else you want to clarify before I continue to risk my life for this mess?"

"Nope, that's about it."

"In that case, if I'm calling the shots, you and I sitting on our heels and waiting for the next heist needs to stop now. We need to start making moves."

Throughout my life, I've always been the one with all the advantages.

I never needed anything because I always had everything. I could count on one-hand situations in my life when I had my back against the wall. The passing of my parents being the most difficult. This was new territory, being the underdog, being outnumbered, not knowing what to do. For what may be one of the first times in my life, I felt like my actions meant something. It was a scary feeling, but it was also exhilarating.

"Most of *The Response*'s heists that we've tracked have been one or two people at a time, more often than not just one. Based on what we know, this group of six, potentially more, is the biggest we've faced. No *Response* member has been caught yet while attempting a heist, which has been one reason getting warrants have been such a challenge," Graham said.

These were facts that both of us needed to remind ourselves of. It was only going to get harder now that *The Response* knows something about my intentions in Boston. It was scary to think about how they know, considering their visit to the bookshop was the first time I ever encountered them. Nonetheless, they must know something. My gut told me that my getting jumped and the JFK manuscript stolen was just the beginning of the personal attacks against me. I wasn't sure what I was going to do about it, but I knew I was becoming more fearful for my safety, and I knew I would need to follow Graham's lead if I had any chance of keeping myself safe.

"What's next, Graham?"

Graham grabbed his napkin, dabbed his lips, and wiped his hands. He put his plate back on the side table, indicating breakfast was over.

"Well, I talked to the analysts right after I got off the phone with the director. They haven't discovered a ton from the video footage we've been sending them, but they've apparently seen that guy that choked you. He's been walking around the Navy Yard late at night. He seems to enjoy the local bars frequently. I'm embarrassed I didn't catch it myself on the live feed from the cameras around the *Constitution*, but that's why I always send the footage to the analysts as soon as it's ready. Always good to have an extra set of eyes on these things to ensure nothing like this gets missed."

"That makes sense. So what else do we know about this guy?"

"We just know he likes to drink. And when he drinks, he does so alone. The analysts have seen him pop up on a few of the recordings I've sent them. He is most often captured walking back from the local bars. The more he kept showing up, the more they paid attention to him. Not once, aside from the night he was at the shop with the other *Response* member, has he not been seen stumbling around town by himself. The *Response* are professionals. They diligently stay under the radar and cover their tracks. This is the first time since we discovered their existence that we've figured out one of their weaknesses. Letting that guy parade around town is a big mistake on their part."

"So, we just start walking around the city going from bar to bar looking for him?"

"You got it. No drinks for us tonight, though, not unless it's to celebrate finding him. Do you have a bar in mind we should start our search at?"

"My family didn't go out much when we were in the city. When we did, it was typically in Beacon Hill. We went to steakhouses and speakeasies for the most part. My grandfather liked dark restaurants where he wouldn't be bothered. Probably not the kind of place I would expect a drunk trying to go."

"Well, the analysts assume *The Response* is staying somewhere near us. Do you know any of the bars in Charlestown?"

"Yeah. The oldest bar in Boston. It's called Warren Tavern. I've never been."

"Warren Tavern it is. Let's plan to go there after dinner time. How about 8 p.m.? Does that work for you?"

"That works."

"Are you planning on opening up the bookshop today?"

"Yeah, heading down there right after I finish this scone. Figure I better eat one while I have the chance. Are you going to come down at all?"

"Not today. I'm going to catch up with the director and update him on the plan for tonight. Then I will need to connect with the analysts after that," Graham said as he headed for the stairs.

I left the living room shortly after—refilling my coffee mug on the way down to the bookshop. Today is the first day since the attack that I've been awake and alert enough to open the bookshop for a full day. It got me excited to see how many customers were coming through. I was optimistic that the now cleaned bloodstain on the front bricks would be a thing of the past. Luckily, the papers didn't seem to catch wind of what had occurred the night I first encountered *The Response*—for better or worse; no one was around when the bookshop was robbed. On a positive note, this meant there was little threat that my "real" customers would feel unsafe. It didn't take a master's degree to recognize that a robbery within the first few weeks of opening your doors was terrible for business.

Pierce's Rare Books on Bunker Hill was back. I flipped the sign to make it official.

Open.

Sixteen

The first full day back in the bookshop went by quickly. There was a decent amount of visitors cycling through, and that kept me busy. I felt like I was pulling books off the shelves and putting them back almost the entire day.

Before I knew it, it was almost 5:30 p.m. and time to close things up. I locked up the shop and headed to the second floor for a quick drink and some dinner. When I walked in, Lucy was taking a look at the bookshop's financials for the month of June.

"Pierce, you know that we lose thousands of dollars every day the shop is open, right?"

Lucy grew up in a lower-middle-class home, similar to Graham's, only in rural England as opposed to Brooklyn. Her parents had a loving marriage, but she often witnessed their relationship get torn apart when they would sit at the dining room table each month trying to figure out how they would pay the bills and if they would have anything left afterward. This is what drove her to send herself to University and study finance. She wanted to help families like her own keep honest jobs and still pay the bills on time. I respected that she used her bright mind for such good, but it was undoubtedly an adjustment when she started paying attention to my monthly bills. She just couldn't fathom the fact that we couldn't spend all of our money even if we tried. We would never be hurting for cash, and all things considered, I didn't spend much money, aside from rare books, art, and whiskey. I was pretty responsible with my finances—given my net worth. At least, I thought I was.

"Didn't you take any finance or accounting courses at that fancy business school?" She asked as she flipped through the reports that she had been updating each day since I opened the shop.

"Hey, people like the books. I want to make sure they make it into the right hands. Hands that will read them—maybe even pass them down to their kids and grandkids."

Lucy sighed and rolled her eyes. She knew what my intent was, and I understood where she was coming from as well. After all these years, her mindset around money wasn't going to change—neither was mine.

"I will pay closer attention to the numbers," I replied.

"You do what you want, Pierce. But the difference between the book's value and what you sell them for is coming out of your personal budget for this month. And at some point, someone is going to take advantage of you and start reselling books you are practically handing out."

Honestly, everything Lucy said was probably a good perspective to keep in mind. Even if I didn't care to hear it at the moment, she was ultimately right. As she usually was.

"Where's Graham?" Lucy asked.

"He's upstairs. We're heading out around 8:00 tonight to try and find the guy who beat me up."

"Does he want to come down here and join us? You know Pierce, it concerns me that you're attempting to track down the exact person that almost killed you—I'd like to make sure Graham agrees that it's safe for you to go."

"It will be okay, Graham wasn't with me last time. I promise you he won't let anything happen to me."

"Fine. I won't fight you about it but I want you to know that everything about this worries me. How do you know that the men who robbed the bookshop will even be at this tavern?"

"We don't know if they'll be at the tavern or not. We just know that one of them is an alcoholic, and we think he's staying somewhere near the Navy Yard. That's the one we think we can catch. Warren Tavern is one of the closest places he would be able to get something to drink."

It was good to have an hour to share a drink of my own with Lucy. Especially now that she had taken a deep breath and cooled down a little about how I handle the operations of the bookshop. Working in the bookshop all day and planning with Graham at night didn't leave much quality time with my wife these days. She understood this would only be the case for a little while. Once we figured out what was going on with *The Response* and things calmed down a little bit—I will owe her big time.

I sipped my glass of wine, and we proceeded to talk more about our days. Lucy shared ideas she had worked on during the past few hours for how the shop could still supply books to customers who may otherwise not be able to afford them while not spending an excessive amount of money. She even wrote up some policies for how we could implement a loan system for the books where people could make payments on the book and eventually make a decision whether or not they wanted to own it later on—sort of like leasing a fancy car. Lucy thought this would be one way for the bookshop to stop risking being taken advantage of by a bad actor. If people were simply leasing the books—then it would be illegal for them to resell them during that period. However, in situations like I had with the young boy buying the Fitzgerald novel, I still would have sold the book outright for $5. There was no doubt in that case that the new owner would do anything with the book besides cherish it—and Lucy certainly agreed with me on that. To Lucy's point, though, in general, I concurred that the loan system would be extremely beneficial. Especially for our adult customers.

"It's about time for Graham and I to meet in the study before we head out to the tavern."

"Okay, it was good to see you, albeit briefly. Be safe," Lucy said as she wrapped her arm around me and kissed the top of my head.

"I really like your idea about leasing the books. Can I get your help estimating what kind of monthly rates we would need to charge?"

"Gladly, only if you promise me you will come back in one piece tonight."

"I promise."

I stood up and grabbed a quarter-zip sweater, which would be enough to keep me warm for a late New England summer night. I pulled the sweater over my head and slipped my loafers back on, they were sitting on the landing outside the door, so I could sneak out at a moment's notice without waking up Lucy at night if needed. When I got up to the third-floor study—Graham was already there waiting for me with all the *Response* materials we had to date sprawled across the table.

"I got some stuff for us to look at before we head out to the bar. What you see here are two profiles. The analysts have now confirmed that the men who jumped you were Toby Morgan and Conan Carlson. Morgan, you know, and Carlson is a retired professional Rugby player from Scotland."

"Yeah, we've discussed Morgan. What's the deal with the rugby player?"

"No idea. He has no record of connection with any of the other *Response* members. That's what we're going to try and figure out tonight."

"Honestly, it makes me feel better that he was a professional rugby player. Hopefully, it will give me more credibility that I wasn't beat up by some lightweight."

"Let's just make sure he doesn't try and take you two rounds tonight. It would be wise not to leave my side."

"You got it, Graham. And you don't hesitate to jump in on my behalf."

"I promised you I always would. Let's head out—it's already a quarter past 8:00."

We walked down the block to the Warren Tavern. It's easy to spot, given its weathered paneling from the years of wear and tear. Cracked seafoam green window sills provided a pop of color amid all the brick. The tavern has been in Charlestown since 1780, and as we walked down Pleasant street approaching the tavern's front entrance, I was reminded of all the history whirling around us. It wasn't just the places themselves or the people that used to frequent them. Something in the air reminds you why what Graham and I were attempting to do was so important, even if no one else understood the long-term impact just yet.

Creak.

The old tavern's door welcomed us with the same sound as the previous thousands of people who had walked through it over the centuries. As we stepped in, I was surprised that my family had never brought me here. It may not have been the same caliber of food and drink they preferred, but I would have thought that their love of history would have overruled their pallets at least once in my lifetime.

Graham started searching the bar.

Nothing.

"You see anything, Pierce?"

"Nope. I don't see his large boots anywhere."

"Let me go talk to the bartender over there and see if he might know more. You stand by the door and see if you recognize anyone in here," Graham said as he went over and flashed his badge.

I held back by the door, but wasn't really serving any purpose. From what I could tell no one in the restaurant looked remotely close to Conan Carlson. Unfortunately, I could only overhear bits and pieces of Graham's conversation with the bartender. From my perspective he didn't seem to be making much progress either.

After a minute or so, Graham walked away from the bar and headed back towards me.

"Alright, let's get out of here."

It was looking like I wouldn't be able to enjoy old Warren Tavern in all of its glory tonight. Graham was quickly on the move. I had to hurry to catch up with him.

"We need to go look at the recorded footage from the security cameras, Pierce. The bartender hasn't seen Conan Carlson in a few days, but that's because he got in a scrape with some locals outside the tavern earlier this week. He hobbled away before the police arrived. The rumor flying around Warren Tavern is that he's staying on a boat docked in the Navy Yard. Apparently, Carlson is famous amongst Rugby fans for his aggression on the pitch—so when he brought that physicality to the tavern, people were alarmed—and rightfully confused about what he was doing there in the first place."

"I didn't even know you could stay on those piers overnight?" I said from behind as I caught up to Graham.

"It's likely one of Reaction Transport's supply boats or something. They probably let them tie on to the dock because they thought they were just moving products and would be departing soon."

"How come the analysts didn't know one of Neville's boats was in Boston?" I asked.

"Not sure. Maybe he just bought it. Probably right after they jumped you—they realized they needed to hide out somewhere else offshore," Graham said.

"Seems to be a pretty obvious place for them to hide. I know there are a lot of boats around here, but still."

"They fooled us, I guess. I'm not quite sure what to think but let's go make sure the security footage from the cameras confirms what the bartender is saying before we check out the piers."

It hurt me to know that we may have let our guard down the past week on my account, but I knew it was true. My bruises were close to healing, but it seemed there could be more trouble ahead. I needed to make a promise to myself now that I wouldn't enter my subsequent encounter with *The Response* in fear, and if anything did go wrong, I would need to protect myself better than I did the first time. The best way to do that was by letting Graham take the lead when it came to this particular portion of the operation.

"Pierce, come on, hurry up. I thought polo players were supposed to be in shape! You can't tell me that even after some time off you can't run for one block!"

We were halfway home already. Graham was at a dead sprint now that we had finished talking. I hadn't played polo in over three months, so I wouldn't say I was in peak shape, but I could get by. I never let myself go too much.

I took off after Graham.

Seventeen

In the study now—Graham worked on pulling up the tapes as I did my best to catch my breath. I haven't sprinted like that in years. Graham started watching and re-watching archived video footage from the Navy Yard piers surrounding the *Constitution* on the split framed screens. After about 30 minutes in front of the monitors, I decided I wasn't adding much value, and Graham wasn't saying anything—I made an old fashioned and grabbed an Ian Fleming novel. I laid on the couch and flipped through the pages.

"Are you just going to sit there and read—or do you want to do something?" Graham asked.

"I could make you a drink?" I mentioned.

"I'm on duty, and so are you. You shouldn't be drinking either."

"Correction, I'm just spending quality time with a friend. You, however, are the one on the clock. I'm a volunteer, remember."

"Whatever. Come here. I think I see Carlson's head at the bottom of this frame."

It was difficult to tell, but you could see enough of his big dome to all but confirm it was Carlson. The man in the frame appeared to be heading towards the *Constitution*. Graham went to the next frame. You could now clearly tell that the lurking man was indeed Conan Carlson. You could also see that he was looking through the quarter gallery window on the ship's port side.

"There we go. Should be all we need to get a warrant to pay Carlson a visit."

"That's all we need?" I asked.

"Looks like intent to steal to me. Plus, he's on the premises of a national historical site after hours. Let me call the director and see if we have the go-ahead to search the boats in the Navy Yard."

"Why do we even need warrants? We're going to have to break so many laws to get these guys. Does it matter if we break this one in particular?"

"I better give the director a heads up regardless, given how stingy everyone has been about letting us investigate Archie Neville's new cabin in Vermont. I need to at least attempt to go by the book when we can," Graham said as he dialed up the director.

The phone rang twice before the director picked up. I couldn't hear what he was saying, but Graham was asking for the free reign to search every boat in Charlestown for Conan Carlson and Toby Morgan. The phone call was short, and Graham showed little expression, so I wasn't sure if we'd just received good or bad news.

"How did it go?"

"We're good to go. He said that he would leave it to our judgment. We just can't search the wrong boat—or civilians will start asking questions. Come on, let's get out of here."

I put my book aside and slammed down the remainder of my drink. No running would be necessary this time. We needed to be diligent, not rushed.

"Here, take this," Graham said as he handed me a Smith & Wesson Magnum revolver handgun fitted with a wooden grip. I'd never touched a gun in my life before this moment. They had always kind of made me nervous. There was a time and place for their use, but I personally never saw why I needed one or why I would ever need to know how to use one. When my father was in Parliament, we had protection around us, so it wasn't like I hadn't seen them or felt a sense of comfort that the people around me would protect me if it came to that. I guess I just never had any personal interest in handling one myself.

"I don't think that's a good idea, Graham. I have no idea how to use a gun. I've never even touched one in my life. Seriously, take this back. I don't need it."

Graham's eyes were like lasers piercing through me.

"It's not for you, Pierce. It's to protect me. Just like I will protect you. Trust me, I don't want to see you try to use that thing any more than you do, but I need you to at least have it on hand in the case things get sketchy. If nothing else, just pull it out and make it look like you know what you're doing. As long as you look confident and in control, then others will believe you. Maybe, one of these days, when we have more time, I can show you how to use it properly, but that time isn't now."

"Okay," I said at first, before realizing I needed to push back and stand up for myself and my values.

"Actually, you know what Graham—take the bullets out of this thing now. I'll keep the gun as a decoy, but I'm never going to take a shot at any of these people. I want you to know that before we leave—shooting guns isn't what I signed up for."

"Fine. Give it here," Graham said as he removed the bullets, "but you better treat this like it's loaded. If you don't convince yourself—you won't convince others."

"Trust me, it feels real enough to me just looking at it."

"Well, here you go then, one empty pistol," Graham said as he handed the weapon back to me.

"Thanks," I said as I uncomfortably tried to figure out where to put this thing. Graham gave me a proper holster, but it was very clunky—so I did away with it when his back was turned. I ended up just sliding it in the back of my shorts. Graham would have been furious with me had he seen it. Not having a holster wasn't the ideal first step towards making *The Response* believe I knew how to handle a gun.

"Okay, let's head out," Graham said as he led the way.

Graham put his suit jacket back on and I snagged my navy Brooks Brothers quarter zip sweater. I suppose our outfits gave away who was the special agent and who was the *New England Monument Adviser*.

We headed back out. At a slower, more controlled pace this time. Strolling through the Training Field, where the lights had just turned on, gleaming off of the Civil War monument. We continued down the street until we approached the Navy Yard piers. From our current vantage point, you could get a good view all around the USS *Constitution*. Unfortunately, no sight of any boats that appeared to belong to Reaction Transport.

"No Reaction Transport boats here—let's head to the other piers past the *Constitution*," Graham said as we continued our march through the Navy Yard.

We walked up and down each pier, which seemed kind of silly because any boat that belonged to Reaction Transport would presumably have some kind of logo on it. But Graham thought if nothing else, we might be able to get an idea of where Carlson had gone after snooping around the *Constitution*.

We weren't coming up with much of anything until we approached pier eight and saw a 40 ft. Sea Ray that we had not previously identified.

"Well, that must be it, they must be using a yacht from Neville's personal fleet," Graham said as he stopped to indicate that neither of us should move any closer without both of us being on the same page.

"The question is whether or not Conan Carlson is in there and if he's sober enough to give us any real information," Graham said.

"You think he'll talk?" I asked.

"He'll talk," Graham said confidently.

"How do you know?"

"Because making people talk is the part of my job I'm best at. Let's plan to enter from the back, I don't see any lights on inside the cabin, so I'm thinking he's not in there."

I didn't want to say it in case Graham would think I was scared, but I was hoping that Carlson wouldn't be on the boat. Having not fully recovered from my prior injuries, I didn't know if I was ready for another scrape just yet, even with Graham by my side. Personally, I assumed that Carlson was not currently on the boat. Given the time of night, I just figured he was still out at the bars. But there was no way of knowing for sure until we got closer. And even if Carlson was at the bars, we still didn't know whether or not Toby Morgan or other *Response* members were inside the yacht. Just because we didn't see lights or any other sign of activity didn't mean that no one was home. We began to methodically approach the boat's port side, heading towards the stern of the yacht. It was still radio silent on the boat. I was feeling much more comfortable with our assumptions. Graham continued to lead the way. I kept an eye out behind us to make sure that no one else was approaching the pier.

"The door is locked. I'm just going to kick it in," Graham said.

Before I could even react, I heard a thud, and the sound of what used to be a pristine wood door flew open towards the cabin. I quickly learned that Graham was collaborative and valued my opinion on some matters, but when it came time to actually catch the thieves—he wouldn't waste time waiting for my thoughts.

Graham flipped on a light. The boat's interior was as expected, just as nice as the exterior, and must have cost well over a hundred thousand dollars. Nicely finished wood tables and leather chairs were scattered around the spacious cabin. Although there were no humans inside at the moment, we found some interesting folders. Inside of which were blueprints of the entire USS *Constitution*. What caught my eye the most, though, was how many different angles and images they had of the captain's cabin.

"Pierce, any significance to these blueprints or images?"

"Not really. Aside from the fact that the area of the ship they appear to have done the most research on is the captain's cabin. The room my grandfather sketched."

"That is interesting. Maybe your grandfather knew something about that room that we don't?"

"If he did, he would have kept it to himself. He didn't trust many people, so if there was anything special about the captain's cabin—I don't think he would have shared it."

I wasn't sure. I knew nothing about the captain's cabin or why my grandfather was interested in sketching it. All I knew about it was the fact that one of my ancestors helped design the cabin and oversaw its construction.

My main concern with *The Response* and their interest in the *Constitution* was that even if they tried to take the thing whole and failed—it would still lead to hundreds of thousands of dollars in damage to the ship. An amount high enough that the US government may pass on restoring it. I knew firsthand how stingy the president was being with financial resources. Obviously, I would be happy to cover these costs, but who knows if the damage done by *The Response* would be beyond what could be salvaged at that point. Maybe that was part of Carlson's assignment—to destroy what he couldn't steal.

Graham searched all of the files he could, but we found nothing that explained the *Prescott* statue's whereabouts. We also didn't find anything that indicated where the rest of *The Response* members were hiding.

In these final moments of looking through the files, we heard what sounded like a giant coming down the pier. The heavy creaks of the boards told us that we were about to have a visitor.

"That's got to be Carlson coming down the pier," I said.

Graham didn't respond but instead pulled out his pistol and peeked around the corner of the door frame that he had kicked in just fifteen minutes ago.

"Yeah, that's his large body coming towards us," Graham said as he shut the door as much as possible and turned off the light so it would appear as though the door was still attached to all of its hinges.

"What should I do?" I stuttered.

"You just protect yourself. Why don't you go towards the front of the cabin and keep your eyes on the entrance? Do you have your gun ready?"

I pulled the empty magnum out of the back of my waistband. If needed, I was ready to act like a federal agent. I moved towards the front of the cabin and hid behind a leather chair with a good view of the door. The creak of the boards was getting louder. I had to calm myself in just a few short breaths. I wasn't sure what would happen

102

next in Graham's plan, but I trusted his instinct to remain behind the door. By now, I could hear the heavy breathing of Carlson just outside the door. You could tell that the lock on the doorknob was turning, but the door was off its hinge. This meant that even though Carlson was more than likely drunk, it would be hard for him not to know that something was up. Graham and I just had to hope that he wouldn't be too quick on his feet and enter the boat with a gun of his own—one with real bullets inside it.

Carlson finally came through the door. You could see the large sweat spots under the armpits of his shirt. He limped his way forward until Graham slammed the opened door back closed. At least, as much as it would slam given that it was already dysfunctional. Throwing his right arm around Carlson, Graham caught a piece of his jaw and continued to coil his arm around the former rugby player's neck. Being the size he was, Graham was just big enough to give the wide-bodied Carlson a run for his money. Carlson may have been a former professional, but Graham was a formidable athlete in his own right. He must have played something competitively, I assumed, American football, but I would need to ask him later.

Graham had Carlson in a tight choke, but Carlson used his frame to bring the fight to the ground, dropping like a bag of rocks to the deck. Carlson did what he could to squirm out of the choke. As both their bodies wrestled on the floor, it was difficult to tell who was in the lead. Carlson appeared to break loose from the choke just enough to catch Graham in the ribs with an elbow. Graham hung on as much as possible, but you could tell Carlson was challenging him. Carlson continually lifted his upper body and slammed his back against the ground as a last-ditch effort to get Graham to release the choke. I began to wonder at what point I was supposed to help Graham. Then I remembered him saying never to intervene unless he was moments from death, which luckily, he wasn't, not yet. I decided I would give him another minute to finish the job. Graham battled for about thirty more seconds before he was able to get on top of Carlson's back. Graham was now pinning his face against the floor. If it weren't for Graham's experience, he wouldn't have been able to get Carlson in a position to put cuffs on him, but he was a pro. He transitioned his hold and got Carlson's arms behind his back. Graham never hesitated for a second. He slipped the cuffs on his wrists and bounced Carlson's upper body against the floor a few times for good measure. Both men looked exhausted from what was probably a two-minute round, but Graham had more gas in the tank. It was easy to tell that Carlson was not in the shape he used to be. The alcohol probably wasn't helping do him any favors. Based on smell alone, Carlson seemed to be sweating pure Jameson.

"What should we do with him, Graham?"

"Interrogate him—but not here. Let's bring him back to the bookshop."

"Why? What's wrong with keeping him here?"

"The rest of his crew might come back here. If we're here at that time—we blow our cover. But if we bring him back to the shop to interrogate him, then they'll just think he's off drunk somewhere. They won't give his absence a second thought."

Carlson was trying to speak up, but as Graham continued to shove his upper half into the ground, it was hard to make out the words from the moans.

"Alright, let's bring him back to the shop then," I said, "but do you think it's a good idea to interrogate him with those big windows out front?"

"We just need to get him back to the shop. Then we can take him up to the study from there," Graham answered.

"I don't want him in my study!" I guess I didn't need to yell. Both Graham and Carlson could hear me perfectly clear.

"It's the most private place to do it, Pierce. So, unfortunately, that's where it needs to happen."

I didn't like it, but Graham was right. This guy didn't deserve to be in the bookshop at all—especially considering his partner stole my father's JFK manuscript while he stomped on my face. On the other hand, the study was the most private place for us to interrogate the perpetrator. I wasn't sure what a full interrogation involved. If it gets even half as rowdy as what I just witnessed, then Graham was right.

The study was the only place it could take place.

"Let's get up!" Graham said as he smooshed Carlson's jowls further into the floorboards before forcing his massive body to get vertical.

Strangely, I was comforted by Graham's force and control of the situation. I felt well protected by Graham and was more assured than ever that he would always have my back. Hopefully, I would never need to pull out this pistol in the back of my waistband.

We left the yacht, only taking the files we found essential so as not to give away to any *Response* members that may enter the boat in the next few hours the idea that anyone other than Carlson had been there.

"What do we do with the blood?"

"Dump some water on it, then smash a bottle of Jameson over it. Make it look like he just had a drunken episode. It shouldn't be too surprising to them. And will hopefully help explain the broken door," Graham said as he looked into Carlson's eyes. "Isn't that right? I'm sure you've smashed a few bottles and broken a few doors in your day."

Carlson turned his head and spat a bloody mix into Graham's eyes. Graham used his shoulder sleeve to wipe away the fluid. Graham applied some extra pressure and led the now handcuffed Carlson out the door and up the pier.

Carlson was pretty quiet on the walk back to *Pierce's Rare Books on Bunker Hill*. Likely, still recovering from his past transgressions. Guess he should've known that karma would get him at some point.

I opened the door and entered the shop first so I could put in the code to unlock the vault door behind the secret bookshelf that led to the stairwell. A panel of books hides the stairs, a feature the carpenters and Graham worked on together. You punch in a code to open the panel. Then there's a vault door with one of those spinning wheel locks that require a fingerprint to unlock. The wheel doesn't actually do anything. It's just for aesthetics. I have no idea why, but it makes it look more secure, and every once in a while, I need to spend money on ridiculous stuff like that just to keep people guessing.

The vault was now open. I let Graham show Carlson to the study on the third floor. We entered, and Graham dropped Carlson onto a chair. The first thing Graham did was grab him a glass of water. This seemed like a nice gesture for someone who you're about to interrogate. I suppose there are times when you have to use force and times when you need cooperation. Agent Graham knew where those lines were and how close he was to them.

"Do you have any questions for our guest, Pierce?" Graham asked.

"Yes, I do, actually. Where's the *William Prescott* statue?"

"I don't know what you're talking about," Carlson answered in his thick Scottish accent.

"The statue. The one you took from the front of the Bunker Hill Monument—where's that statue?"

"I don't know. I don't know what you're talking about."

"Okay then," Graham leaned forward, "What were you doing by the USS *Constitution*?"

"The big ship? I was just looking at it, the biggest sailing ship I've ever seen," Carlson said.

"Don't play dumb with me, Carlson. You know the significance of "that big ship," now start talking, or do you need me to tighten these handcuffs a little more," Graham said as he made a move for Carlson's wrists.

"Yeah, I know it's important. Does that mean I'm not allowed to look at it? Isn't it a museum?" Carlson responded.

"Most people are allowed to just look at it. That's not what you were doing, though, was it? Just looking? No, you were planning to take something off that ship, weren't you?" Graham asked forcefully.

"Why would I do that?"

Not sure if I was supposed to speak up now, but I did.

"Because you're taking symbols of the Revolution and War of 1812," I said.

"What?" Carlson answered with a perplexed look as if he genuinely didn't know what he was doing or what any of what I just said even meant.

Graham took over again.

"Let me ask you a simpler question then. How much is Archie Neville paying you?"

Carlson paused. I'm no FBI agent, but it looks like Graham just stumped him.

"How do you know Admiral Neville?"

"How do you know him?!" Graham repeated as he tossed a wooden chair across the room.

Carlson's head dropped down to the floor and turned away from Graham's eyes.

"CARLSON!" Graham pounded his fist on the oak desk and screamed in Carlson's ear.

"Fine! I met Neville two years ago in London," Carlson finally answered.

"London, huh, tell me more about your relationship with him."

"I met the Admiral at a pub in London. He is friends with the owner of my former rugby club, it turns out, and he came up and bought me a drink. He was asking me about what I wanted to do after I retired from rugby. We had a big international tournament coming up that was probably going to be my last with the Scottish national team, so I was starting to think about what I wanted to do with the rest of my life."

"And what did you want to do?" Graham asked more calmly.

"I wasn't sure what I wanted to do after rugby. That was the problem. The Admiral said to give him a call when the time came for me to retire. He said that he would take care of me if I were interested in working for him."

"So, after the tournament, you called him and started working for him?" Graham asked.

"Not exactly, I called him, and we talked about what I could do for him. I figured I would be working a desk job for his transportation company or traveling some and making sales. When I talked to him, though, he brought up a special project he was working on that was separate from the company's day-to-day operations. Whatever it was, he was funding it on his dime but still using some of the company's resources. Mainly taking personnel, he felt would be a good fit."

"And that's when you started working for *The Response*?"

You could tell that Carlson was scared and visibly upset. He didn't want to rat out Neville, the man who gave him a career when others were tossing him to the curb.

"No, not that night. It wasn't until a few months later when Neville met me in Scotland. He brought along his right hand, Toby Morgan. Toby is much closer in age to me. I was glad I might have a few men to work with that could become my friends. Plus, they both came to Scotland to meet with me. That gesture meant a lot to me."

"What did they tell you the job would be?"

"I can't tell you that."

"Listen, Conan, I know your name, I know the people you work for, I know where you sleep, I have eyes on you now. You need to recognize that you still have a lot of life to live, and you can have your life back, but only if you cooperate with me. Otherwise, we'll be watching your every move for the rest of your life. You might never leave this study."

It took Carlson a solid fifteen seconds to gather himself. He seemed to be weighing the pros and cons of being wanted by the FBI versus Archie Neville. Either way, he knew he was pissing someone off that he didn't want to see pissed off.

"I didn't know all the details, but I knew it would be a lot more physically taxing than I had expected. It sounded more like a security job. They wanted to know if I knew how to shoot a gun—which I did from hunting with my pop growing up. They wanted to know if my body was up to it. They had even researched my medical history and brought to the surface some old rugby injuries. They wanted to know if I could still run people down. Which I had proven I could."

"That's all you knew when you said yes? That the job would involve providing security for Neville and that he would pay you in cash?"

"Yes, that's all I knew."

"So, you took the job for the money?"

"I took it for the adventure. He told me I would get to travel to America with Toby. My job would be to protect Toby on the road. Toby and I hit it off, so I thought it would be a good time, at least for a few years, until I figured out what I wanted to do with the rest of my life."

"You're positive you didn't know anything about what Archie Neville and Toby Morgan were planning to do when you got involved with them? You didn't know they were trying to steal historical monuments from New England?" Graham asked.

"No, I didn't. I swear to you. I could barely show you New England on a map at the time I accepted the offer," Carlson answered.

It was weird, but I kind of believed Carlson's ignorance. Maybe that's why I would never make it working as a special agent for the FBI. I'm way too prone to believing people.

"Okay, let me ask you another question then." Graham was not quite as gullible. "How long have you been in New England?"

"About a year."

"And for that year, while all of these heists were happening, like the other night when you stole that manuscript from this very bookshop, you never thought to yourself, "hey, maybe I'm helping bad people?" You never thought to stop working for Neville?" Graham probed.

Carlson was silent.

Graham was the first to speak back up.

"Listen, Conan. You will be in prison for a while no matter what, but it's up to you for just how long you want to be locked away. Pierce and I have friends that can help ease your sentence, but only if you tell us a few things. For example, what were you doing near the USS *Constitution*? Where is the *Prescott* statue? And where is the JFK manuscript?"

Carlson was sweating profusely. His Scottish complexion began shifting between shades of red, pink, and pale as Graham interrogated him. Graham pushed the glass of water back towards him, indicating that it was safe to take a drink before responding.

"There was no plan to take the USS *Constitution*. Neville sent one of his boats there as a backup to protect the *Prescott* statue. He simply gave us the green light to check it out if we saw it unguarded. The other night I walked by, and no one was there, so I thought I would take a peek inside."

"Why do these folders from the boat indicate that you were specifically trying to search the captain's cabin?"

"Those folders aren't orders. They're more like guidelines to follow.

We have them for every city and town throughout New England. They're simply a description of artifacts and monuments that the Admiral has an interest in obtaining. He doesn't just give us the freedom to take whatever we want. He has a plan about what he views as most valuable. Whatever *Response* members are in that city or town—they receive a specific set of folders. I didn't come to Boston to search the ship. It's just the fact that I was going to be in Boston, and the ship was on the Boston list."

"So what part of the ship does Archie Neville deem valuable?" Graham asked.

"I don't know. Honestly, I don't. But, as I said, I didn't even know the ship was so important until I met the two of you."

Carlson was opening up ever since Graham made mention of a deal. I found it odd that Carlson didn't press Graham more on what the deal would entail, but I think the questions were starting to cause him to crack regardless of the terms. This was good news for us.

"These folders—where are the rest of them?" Graham asked.

"I don't know. When the Admiral gives members an assignment, he sends Toby to deliver the files. It's not until Toby receives them that I even know about their existence. I'm not even sure if Toby knows where they're stored. It could be that the Admiral keeps them somewhere only he knows about. I usually don't even get to see the files myself. My main job is to protect Toby, not search for the items listed in the folders. It was just a slow night, and Toby didn't need me, so I went ahead and tried to be helpful by checking out the ship. Now I wish I hadn't."

"Okay, I believe you. So, where is the *Prescott* statue? Because I assume that if you were left alone tonight, that means the other *Response* members are up to no good somewhere else."

Carlson started mumbling to himself.

"Where is it, Conan?" Graham repeated.

Again, no direct response.

"Where's the statue? This is the final time I'm going to ask," Graham said as he made sure Carlson caught a glimpse of his pistol.

"It's already on another one of the Admiral's yachts, much bigger than the one in the Charlestown Navy Yard. The statue is being held in the cabin of the yacht until it's safe to deliver to the Admiral's cabin."

"The cabin in Vermont?"

Conan Carlson nodded his head in agreement.

"I see. It's pretty difficult to get a life-sized statue to Vermont from Boston without anybody knowing. How do they plan to get it there?" Graham asked.

"Helicopter," Carlson confirmed.

My eyes widened, as did Graham's. I guess that was one way to do it.

"Where's this helicopter going to be landing?"

"Near that island with the high walls. Some kind of old fort, I think?"

"What?" Graham was confused.

This was my place to chime in. I had seen blueprints of Fort Warren in one of the files Carlson left out.

"Those walls are called Fort Warren and are located on George's Harbor Island. It got its name after Dr. Joseph Warren, who died right out there," I said as I pointed towards the Bunker Hill monument. "The fort was used as a prisoner camp during the Civil War. It used to be full of Confederate officers, but now it remains largely unused except by tourists and Neville, apparently. Do you know Sylvanus Thayer—the man who founded West Point? He was one of the engineers in charge of the fort's construction," I said.

I thought about providing more details regarding the fort, but Graham gave me a look that said he only needed the fort's name, not its origin story. I let him continue.

"So, the rest of *The Response* members are at this fort?" Graham asked Carlson.

"Or close by," Carlson said, "they're waiting for the right time when no one is around to move the shipping crate that the statue is in from the inside of the yacht to the island so the helicopter can pick it up. There's no helicopter pad on the yacht, so they had to find an area to land. This fort has multiple options, apparently."

"Pierce, how long will it take us to get to Fort Warren from here?"

"Not long. We need a boat, though," I said to Graham.

Graham looked over at Carlson and reached out his hand for the keys to the Sea Ray.

Carlson handed them over.

"Oh yeah, one last thing before we get out of here. Who has the JFK manuscript?" I asked once again.

"We sent it to the Admiral—he has it now."

Eighteen

Still in cuffs, Carlson was escorted by Graham back to the Sea Ray. I followed close behind. Luckily, Graham knew how to handle a boat properly because I certainly didn't. I've owned a lot of boats in my life but always had a captain to guide them. We climbed back on board. We were relieved that the boat appeared to be in the same state we'd left it. Unfortunately, this meant the cabin still wreaked of blood, sweat, and Irish whiskey.

Graham fired up the motor. He let the handcuffed Carlson sit up towards the bow. He didn't treat him like a criminal. Well, except for during the interrogation, but once Graham got the information he needed, he treated Carlson with similar respect as he would anyone else. I admired this about Graham.

We took off. I guided Graham to the location where Carlson indicated we could expect to find the other yacht that belonged to *The Response*. This was the boat we hoped had the *Prescott* statue somewhere in its cabin. Graham got us out on the water away from the city in short order, and it wasn't long before you could see the concrete walls of Fort Warren in the distance.

The mid-nineteenth century fort sits on about 40 acres of land. There was plenty of space for Neville to land his helicopter and quickly escape with the statue. We cruised along until we were a few miles out, at which time we chose to slow down significantly so we could quietly approach the fort. As we approached, you could not see much of anything except for the tall granite walls that formed the shape of a large pentagon. It looked like we would need to circle the island and pray that *The Response* yacht was not missing in action. Carlson said that the evacuation plan was supposed to be taking place tonight, but it would depend on many factors as to when Archie Neville would arrive to pick it up. Even Carlson didn't know the exact time *The Response* was expecting Neville. At least, that's what he was claiming. We chose to believe that he was telling the truth.

As we looped around the island, we caught our first glimpse of the other boat. I've seen quite a few nice yachts throughout my life, but this had to have been one of the nicer ones. Even from afar, its sheer size was impressive. It was probably 80 - 90 feet and was certainly big enough to conceal a statue, like the one of *Colonel William Prescott*, without attracting much attention. That is, outside of the expected attention a large yacht would typically receive. We continued, getting closer and closer until we started to see a few presumed *Response* members head out to the bow. They wore black military special operations-type uniforms that clung close to their bodies and included many pockets and compartments for their weapons and gadgets. The uniforms were futuristic looking. All of them were wearing night-vision goggles that shifted from shades of purple to blue depending on where they turned their heads. I can't imagine Carlson fitting in such a suit. These must be their premiere operations guys.

"What are those?" Graham asked Carlson.

"Those are *Response Raiders*."

"How come you weren't wearing one of those suits when we found you?" Graham asked.

"I'm not a *Raider* since I don't come from a military background. So, I'm one of the few that doesn't need to wear the suit. Admiral

Neville, Toby Morgan, and I, none of us wear *The Response Raider* uniform. Toby could wear it if he wanted to. He certainly has the skill set, but he prefers not to most of the time."

"And what is the skill set that it takes to be a *Raider*?" I asked.

"Trained special operational skills, I guess…" Carlson said as he shrugged his shoulders, not being sure how else to define it.

We slowly approached the mega yacht. It was even more impressive up close than it was from afar. As we got closer, we could see two *Raiders* on the bow and two more protecting the stern.

I decided to speak up again.

"How many *Raiders* are on this boat, Carlson?"

"Last I heard, there were supposed to be four plus Toby. Toby is the head of the *Raiders* and oversees all of their operations."

It occurred to me on our trip over to the fort that Carlson may have genuinely had no intention to play a role in the thefts of historical monuments. Maybe, Archie Neville caught him at the right time, offered him financial freedom for life with the salary he was willing to pay, and allowed Carlson to travel. And that was the extent of why Carlson accepted the offer. If that was the case, it worked well in our favor because although reluctant to share details at first, it was now becoming clear that Carlson's allegiances were to Archie Neville the man, not to *The Response*'s mission. As long as he didn't think he was betraying Neville, he was willing to speak up about *Response* related operations. It seemed he felt comfortable enough with us now that he would continue to answer questions if approached correctly. Knowing this, I asked another question that had been on my mind.

"Carlson, the FBI analysts believe there to be around 50 members of *The Response* total. It's my feeling that there are more. Am I correct in that assumption?"

"Yes. I don't know how many *Raiders* there are now because the numbers are increasing quickly, but it's well beyond 50. I mean, the last meeting at the Admiral's cabin had at least 100 *Raiders*."

I looked over at Graham. His brows raised. I figured there were many more members than we had initially thought based on how Carlson spoke about the *Raiders* versus non-*Raiders* and how he talked about Neville recruiting from his over twenty thousand employee company. Reaction Transport alone was bound to produce at least a few hundred qualified *Response* members.

We slowed down as much as we could and maintained our distance from *The Response* yacht. We didn't want *The Response* to think we were anything other than a ship passing in the night. You could tell that each *Raider* was carrying some form of combat rifle that looked like it could burst bullets through my chest at an alarming rate.

The question now is what we should do next?

So far, our focus has been on merely finding *The Response*. If nothing else to confirm their existence, which I did the day Alexander Andrews came into the bookshop, and again the night I met Conan Carlson and Toby Morgan. On the other hand, the *Raiders* were an element that we weren't expecting, at least not armed like they were.

Now that we had found them and knew that the *Prescott* statue was nearby, we just needed a plan to get it back.

How were we going to get on that yacht without getting shot?

Nineteen

As we began to pull into the line of sight—we faced a decision.

Since there were only three of us on board, including Carlson, they outnumbered us no matter how you looked at it. We weren't as concerned with the extra bodies as we were with the combat weapons. We also didn't know if Toby Morgan was hiding somewhere else on the boat in addition to the *Raiders*. We were working off of the assumption that Morgan was somewhere below deck. This meant another layer of defense we would have to account for before making a move for the *Prescott* statue.

I moved away from the bow with Carlson and went to discuss with Graham, who had the wherewithal to cut the engine before we got any closer to the yacht.

"Any ideas about how we should approach this, Graham? I know you gave me this pistol, but I don't think we want to get into a fight with these guys."

"Yeah, you think! I don't know what to do. How big is the statue again?"

"Big enough that we will most likely need to borrow that yacht to transport it back to the Navy Yard."

"Okay, let's think, we need a plan to steal the boat from the *Raiders*. Worst case scenario, it's 2 v. 6, and at best, it is 3 v. 4."

"How do you figure?" I asked.

"Well, if Carlson would be willing to side with us, then that would make three. If he sides with them and Toby Morgan is in the cabin, then we are looking at 2 v. 6, which is not a place I want to be, but the situation may call for it."

"Do you think Carlson would be willing to help us?"

"Maybe, it doesn't seem like he's all that invested in *The Response*'s mission. It might just be talk, but from what he says, it seems like they left him in the dark on a lot of information about their mission. As much as he feels loyalty towards Archie Neville, he's a smart enough guy to realize that Neville hung him out to dry and withheld important information. With as much as Carlson has told us already, I can't say I blame him."

"But can we trust him?"

"We don't have enough time to figure out if we can trust him or not. Even if it's 50/50, we need to go for it. How else can we get on that boat without getting shot unless Carlson is on our side."

"You want me to talk to him?"

"Yeah, that's a good idea. He seems to have a thing for British billionaires."

"Give me a break, Graham," I said as I headed back over to the other side of the boat to continue my chat with Conan Carlson.

"Well, Conan, I'm sure tonight isn't going as you thought it would," I said as he stared right into my eyes. It could be that he was inspecting the bruising still leftover on my face from his boot.

"Listen, I want you to know that I'm sorry for what I did to you. When I took this job, I thought I was just supposed to be protecting people. I never imagined I would be the one starting the conflicts. That's not the person I am. I understand you probably don't believe me. I wouldn't believe me if I were you, but it's true."

He was right, it was difficult for me to think that the person who tried to cave my face in was decent at heart, but I had to trust him. I had to believe that people might surprise you if you give them the opportunity. There have certainly been times in my own life when I have required this same kind of grace, maybe not to the extent of the current situation with Conan Carlson, but that wasn't the point.

"You know what, Conan, you're correct in the fact that I don't believe you're a better man than you were a week ago, and frankly, I don't trust that you're being fully honest with Graham and me. With that said, I'm willing to allow you to surprise me. If you're truly the kind of man you claim to be, then you'll help us take down those *Raiders*. You'll help us get the statue, and most importantly, you'll help us find my father's manuscript from President Kennedy. The same manuscript that you stole in the first place. You help us accomplish all these things, and I'll forgive you, but you can't just apologize as if nothing happened between us. I need to see it in your actions."

"Let's say I do help you. By the way, I hope it's clear that I've been helping you this whole time. I already told you that ever since Morgan and I jumped you, I've been one foot out the door. I've been drinking the whole time—trying to deal with how bad I felt. But if I continue to help you, will you protect me from the *Raiders*? Because there's no doubt in my mind that as soon as they're done with you, they'll come after me. They may even come after me first, but one thing is certain, they will not stop until they get their revenge."

"Well, let me put it to you this way, Conan. If you want to redeem yourself for your past transgressions, *The Response* doesn't seem like the kind of people that will allow you to do it. You've given us helpful information, extremely helpful. However, since we're already outnumbered, even with you, we'll need more than just information. We'll need your physicality and protection. We'll need your full commitment."

Graham didn't add anything to the conversation, but I knew he heard me loud and clear from the helm.

I waited for Carlson to respond, but in the back of my head, I wasn't sure if it mattered if he decided to help us or not. No matter what, we still lacked the power that *The Response* had. If we had Carlson on our side, the best we could hope for would be to have him play some kind of double agent and at the very least help us get on the boat.

"Okay," Carlson said quietly.

"Okay?" I repeated.

"Okay, I'm in. I'll join you and Graham, but you have to trust me. I want Graham to trust me too. No more interrogations, and no more doubting me when I give you information. You both need me. Act like I'm a part of your team now. Act like I'm on your side."

"We won't just act like it, Conan. You are a part of our team now."

"Are you going to take me out of these cuffs?"

I didn't have the ability to release the cuffs, so I went up to chat with Graham.

"Not sure if you heard, but he's in," I confirmed with Graham.

"Do you trust him?"

"Yeah, I trust him."

"I guess if you can trust the man that almost killed you—then I should be able to trust him as well."

Graham gave me the keys for the cuffs. I released Carlson. At the same time, Graham came down and joined us on the bow. We floated just around the bend of the island to get back to an area that was out of sight of the *Response Raiders*. We could still see them when we turned in a particular direction, but we stayed out of their direct line of sight. At least we hoped we were out of sight. Ultimately, we had no idea just how effective their fancy night-vision goggles were.

"Let's assume there are five people on the yacht, four *Raiders* plus Toby Morgan. With the four *Raiders* armed, we will not be able to approach the yacht via the boat. We'll need to tie off on this side of the island and approach on foot. Do you have your gun ready, Pierce? You may need to use it this go around."

"Yeah, I got it," I said—playing into the false narrative that my gun could actually do anything.

Conan Carlson, on the other hand, was not armed at all. I got the sense that Graham wanted to keep it that way until he earned his stripes.

"Do you have something for me?" Carlson asked.

"No. We don't," Graham replied.

"How am I supposed to protect myself?"

"We'll protect you. Plus, as far as the *Raiders* are concerned, you're still one of them, remember?"

Carlson nodded in agreement.

"So, we approach by land, then what?" I asked since I deferred to Graham on all strategy matters, especially when armed assassins were involved.

"When were they expecting you to arrive tonight, Carlson?" Graham asked.

"Not until after midnight. I just needed to be here in time for when the helicopter arrived. Then the *Raiders* and I were supposed to get both boats to Cape Cod."

"Good. It's only 11:30 right now. There will be a brief moment when the *Raiders* will be off their guard due to you arriving earlier than expected. Do you think they'll be surprised to see you this far in advance to midnight?"

"I would assume. I'm still supposed to be doing recon near the *Constitution*. I was instructed not to leave the Navy Yard until much closer to the expected arrival of the Admiral's helicopter."

"Great. We'll have you go on-board first," Graham said as he pointed at the former rugby star. "Then, during that brief moment, when the *Raiders'* attention is taken away, Pierce and I will enter the yacht on the opposite side and work our way inside the cabin," Graham looked over at me and continued. "Pierce, we'll need to be precise in our movements and dead silent. It's hard enough sneaking by operatives like this without being on the water. Navigating a boat often means unexpected noises. Hopefully, it will sound like any other noise caused by the water, but that will only get us so far until they know they have visitors."

I nodded my head in agreement. If I was going to turn back—I should've done so days ago. Graham needed a partner at this moment more than ever, and I was his best option. His only option.

I stared at *The Response Raiders*, peering around the premises with their purple hazed optics that continued to shift colors with every movement of their heads.

"Pierce, there's a hitch coming up on the starboard side. Why don't you tie us off, and we can jump onto the dock."

We climbed off the boat. We were on what I would consider the front side of the island. During the day, ferry boats of tourists dock on this side. Past visiting hours now, there weren't any other boats or people on the island. *The Response Raiders* were around the bend on the northern side. If nothing else, approaching via the dock was much more forgiving on our attire than if we had tried to swim, Graham in his suit, and I in my loafers. I wouldn't say we had the same kind of state of the art equipment as the *Raiders*. At least I was comfortable, though. No amount of equipment, no matter how high-tech, would make me an actual operative. If it came down to a firefight, we weren't going to win. What we would have to do was outsmart them. Surely, I could do that in a pair of loafers. That's the whole reason the director wanted me in this position in the first place.

We walked down the old dock as quietly as we could. Upon making it to the grass, we increased our speed to get to the fort's outer concrete wall at a faster rate. Slamming our backs against the wall as the sweat began to gleam off of all of our foreheads. It was the second day of July now, and the humidity wasn't cutting us any breaks. Taking the bottom of my shirt, I quickly tried to dry my face. We pressed forward towards the northernmost wall. You could see the imprints of our bodies as the sweat smeared across the concrete. Graham pulled out his gun and peered around the corner of the wall.

"Yep, still out there," Graham said.

"They won't leave the ship," Carlson mumbled.

"Thanks for that, Carlson," Graham responded sarcastically.

Carlson began to walk around the side of the wall so that he would be in plain sight of *The Response*.

"What're you doing, Carlson? Get back behind the wall," Graham demanded.

"I'm going to talk to them. Don't worry about me."

Except, we remained very worried about him. Don't get me wrong, Carlson and I had a good talk on the boat. But I don't think Graham felt the same level of trust in Carlson that I was beginning to, and not listening to his order to get back behind the wall was another strike. Carlson continued walking towards *The Response* yacht without looking back at us. He showed little interest in whether we were following him or not. I sure hope I'm not wrong about him. He raised his hand and gave a wave. *The Raiders* lifted their goggles and greeted their comrade. They pulled that yacht closer to the island so Carlson could make his way on board. At least having the yacht closer to land would make things a little easier when Graham and I attempted to make our entrance.

I held my breath and waited. If Carlson were going to throw us under the bus, now would be the time to do it. Luckily, he seemed to be proceeding, as we hoped he would. Not only engaging the two *Raiders* within sight but gathering the entire team of four in one location on the yacht. Carlson worked his way to the back of the boat on the starboard side. We could no longer see him or any of the *Raiders*. It was a large yacht, after all. We hoped that Toby Morgan would soon join them on deck, but we weren't going to assume he left the cabin until we knew for sure. Graham reached back, grabbed my wrist, and gave me a head nod that we should continue onward around the corner of the wall.

We continued our silent trek, now beginning to cross the grass and sand, making our way towards the port side of the bow of the boat until we were close enough to grab hold of it and scale the side. The sheer size of the boat allowed us to hang from the frame without touching the land or water. Again, good news for my loafers and Graham's suit. Graham led the way and shimmied until we were parallel to the cabin door. Pausing as we tried our best to listen in on Carlson's discussion with the *Raiders*. The conversation seemed light, certainly no talk of strategy or anything else of significance for that matter. Unfortunately, none of the voices belonged to Toby Morgan. I remembered his voice from the other night. Despite my presumed concussed state after getting kicked by Carlson, I could still hear Morgan when he thanked me for the manuscript. The other confirming variable was the shoes they were wearing. I lifted my body slightly so I could see all of the shoes on deck. Four pairs of combat boots and Carlson's boots that still had my blood residue on the right toe confirmed that Morgan was still below deck. That's if he was on the boat at all.

Graham took a look over his shoulder and made eye contact before putting his Marine caliber strength to work and pulling himself up, transitioning from an overhang pull-up to a tricep dip position, before he slipped through the bars connected to the deck of the yacht. My pull-up was less graceful, but still got the job done.

We were both on board.

The door to the cabin was open, but quietly making our way down the stairs would be a challenge. Carlson continued to keep the *Raiders* engaged for us. The steps made few sounds, and I thanked God that the yacht was brand new, so the floorboards did not creak.

The cabin was spacious, filled with luxurious furniture and other modern interior designs. A giant U-shaped couch wrapped around a large oak table in the center of the room. Complete with a minibar stocked with high-end vodka located directly behind it. There was no sign of Toby Morgan, but there was a closed-door with light peeking through the bottom crack.

"He's in that room, Pierce. Pull out your pistol and get behind me," Graham instructed with a whisper.

That was undoubtedly what I planned to do anyway, minus the "pull out my pistol" portion. I mean why wouldn't I let the trained special agent lead from the front? If we were going into a library, a museum, or a church, maybe I would consider leading the way.

Graham went to turn the knob.

Locked.

He cocked his head back in my direction with a scowl. The last thing we wanted to do was make noise. We couldn't kick the door in this time, or *The Raiders* would be alerted of our presence.

"What do you need?" A voice came from beyond the door. It was Morgan.

"What?!" Morgan repeated with a louder tone this time.

Graham led me into the room that shared a dividing wall with Morgan's.

We waited to hear if the door would swing open, but it didn't.

The next thing we heard was heavy footsteps making their way down the stairwell.

It was undoubtedly Carlson. I wondered if he knew we were down here. Surely, he had assumed we had made it onto the boat by now.

Knock. Knock.

"What!" Morgan yelled once again.

"Hey, it's Conan," Carlson barked back at the door.

"Conan? What're you doing here? One second, I'll get the door. You should've spoken up the first time," Morgan responded.

I could hear the lock being played with, followed by the opening of the door. There weren't any words shared for a few seconds. It sounded like they embraced each other in a hug or something. The door closed again, and the lock was re-adjusted. Graham put his ear to the wall but only until the two men started talking. At that point, you could hear them pretty well through what must have been a thin wall.

"When does the Admiral get here?" Carlson started things off.

"Should be here any minute now. I thought you weren't supposed to come back until after we moved the statue? Were you able to find anything out on the *Constitution*?" Morgan asked.

"No I wasn't. I came early because I needed to talk to the Admiral."

"Did you make it into the captain's cabin?"

"No."

"So, we still don't know where that hidden panel is?"

"No, not yet. I tried my best but it wasn't the right time. There were still a few people walking around the ship that could have seen me."

"The Admiral isn't going to be happy about this. We have to find that panel. It's the only way he will know for certain what it's hiding."

"Which is what again?"

"I don't know. Some kind of box that was supposedly hidden inside the ship when it was built. But the Admiral won't tell me what's inside said box. Maybe he doesn't even know himself."

"Well, I doubt he would be risking all of this if it wasn't something of great value."

"True. Whatever it is, Admiral Neville is growing more impatient by the day about it. He updated Plan B to include the destruction of the USS *Constitution* by sunset on the 4th of July if he doesn't find what

125

he's after. Can you believe that? Destroying the USS *Constitution* just because you either find or don't find whatever supposed valuables are hidden inside it—seems a little sinister even for him. Not to mention what would happen if anyone ever found out he was responsible for it all—Reaction Transport would be doomed, not to mention *The Response* that is just now starting to deliver some results."

"Let's hope that doesn't happen. There is something else I need to warn you about."

"What's that?"

"Pierce Spruce is searching for us."

"How would Pierce Spruce know about us or our plans? I thought we knocked some sense into him the other night. Do we need to pay his rare bookshop another visit?"

"He came and found our yacht in the Navy Yard. He had some federal agent with him who was interrogating me for information."

"I was wondering where all the swelling in your face came from. Did you tell them anything? How did you escape?"

"I led them here. They're on the other side of the island as we speak. I figured that couldn't hurt based on the plans for tonight."

"Smart, Carlson. Risky—but smart."

"Thank you. I hope the Admiral will be pleased."

"He will definitely be more pleased about you leading Pierce Spruce here then he will be that you weren't able to sneak onto the *Constitution*. But as long as we can execute Plan B then it won't be an issue."

"That was my hope—I can't afford to blow this operation."

"It will be fine. Plan B will work. I wish we would have just finished the job at the bookshop. I know Admiral Neville didn't want us to because of how things ended with Spruce's parents in Newport all those years ago. But things are different now. And we had a great opportunity to erase Pierce Spruce from the equation. Now that we didn't, it sounds like he's trying to stick his nose in our operation."

"Why do you think the Admiral didn't just give you the greenlight?"

"He's worried he may need some information from him to find this stupid hidden panel that he's so interested in or something like that. I don't know. I think he just wants to take care of Pierce Spruce himself."

When Toby Morgan finished, there was a pause. That pause continued for quite some time. During that pause, I felt the life flush from my body. It wasn't the kind of anger that made your face red and led you to clench your fists. This was an anger, a rage that I had not experienced since the day of my parent's death. My sweat was no longer warm and sticky. Instead, it poured out of me at an icy temperature and caused my body heat to plummet. I was still breathing but at an irregular pace. If what I heard was true, then Toby Morgan not only confirmed that *The Response* had a bounty on my head but that Archie Neville was in some way responsible for the death of my parents.

I knew they were murdered. I knew they were murdered all along, but no one listened to me. Those detectives were either wrong or paid off by Neville. Maybe, they weren't even real detectives at all. These questions could have been answered years ago if the director had just listened to me when I told him my parent's death was no accident and that he needed to have the FBI investigate it further.

Graham reached over and grabbed my wrist. He shook it for a second. It was as if he was consoling me and telling me to snap out of it all at the same time. After all, a man who wanted me dead was less than ten feet away.

I did my best to control myself. There would be a time to dig deep into the news I just heard but now wasn't it. I needed to be present and, in the moment, to help Graham. I needed to be as sharp as possible if we were going to make it out of here. With the statue, the manuscript, or simply with our lives. I just wanted off this yacht.

"Well, Carlson."

We could hear Toby Morgan speak back up, I tried my best to remain calm and listen in.

"The Admiral should be arriving shortly. We need to make sure that the statue is ready for him and that he is aware we need to pursue Plan B before Pierce Spruce learns more."

Both Toby Morgan and Conan Carlson left the room and headed upstairs to the deck. I could feel vomit shooting up my throat that took everything in me to keep down.

The stakes were rising.

Twenty

"Well, that was dark. I'm so sorry about your parents, Pierce. But, we won't let their death be in vain."

"Thanks, but there's no need to be sorry. I always knew that my parent's death wasn't an accident. I just didn't know who was responsible. Now I know that it was Archie Neville, which brings some sort of closure, I suppose."

"Even closure doesn't always make things easier."

"True. The best I can do now is make sure that we stop Neville and his gang of thieves."

"Speaking of, do you have any idea what information they were referencing?" Graham asked.

"No idea, but it seems like whatever this "panel" is in the ship's cabin—is likely the same one my grandfather was trying to find when he first took me to the USS *Constitution*."

"Do you remember anything your grandfather said or did on that day? Did he share anything with you that seemed out of the ordinary?"

My head went back and hit the wall as I stared at the ceiling and tried to remember my first time visiting the USS *Constitution*, my only time prior to this trip.

"Honestly, nothing out of the ordinary from that day stands out. The only strange thing that happened was at the end of that week when he was sending me on my way back home to London—he handed me one of his pocket notebooks and told me to make sure I gave it to my father as soon as I saw him."

"Did you look inside the notebook at all?"

"Not really, it was just a bunch of notes and sketches. But, as I said, my grandfather constantly had his nose in those little notebooks. It drove my grandmother crazy!"

"The notebook he gave you before your flight. Any chance it was the same one that had the sketches he drew of the USS *Constitution*'s cabin?"

"Possibly. I can't focus on flights Graham, they have scared me since before I can remember. I was just clenching my eyes shut and hoping I made it home in one piece with the notebook still in my pocket. Which I did—I delivered it to my father as instructed and never thought about it again until now."

Clunk! Clunk! Clunk!

You could hear the *Raiders* boots moving quickly around the deck.

Before Graham could respond to the information I had just given him, he rose from his seated position and went to look up the stairwell.

There was a faint buzzing sound that was growing louder by the second until it became blistering loud.

It had to be Neville's helicopter.

"Neville is landing. Let's see if they leave the boat to go greet him."

That's exactly what the *Raiders*, Morgan, and Carlson all did. As soon as the helicopter cut off, you could hear them leave the boat to greet their "Admiral."

"Graham, should we go up and check things out?"

"Let's go to the top step and make sure everyone is off the boat. I think now would be a good time to bail. My gut tells me we don't have much to gain from being on the yacht any longer. The statue isn't on the boat, and we risk a lot by staying here with a minimal reward if any."

"Should we check Morgan's room for any other documents?"

"He locked it. I would need to kick in the door. At this point, I'm not willing to risk it if it means staying on the boat any longer. Especially now that we know they have a bounty out on you."

"Okay, I can appreciate that."

We made our way up the stairs. No one was on deck anymore, so we decided to hop off and head back for the fort to gather our thoughts. The helicopter had landed on the northeastern side of the island. We could see a large moving crate next to the landing zone.

"I bet you that's our statue," Graham said.

"Are they going to hook it up to the helicopter and bring it to Vermont?"

"Would be a long way to travel with that thing dangling down from a helicopter. I'm not sure how that would work without bringing unwanted attention. Even at this time of night, people would still think that was odd."

"Why would Neville bring his helicopter here then?"

"Don't know, maybe Neville just wanted to come to check it out."

You could see Carlson's big body, even from the other side of the island. He was talking to Neville, or "Admiral Neville" as *The Response* insisted on calling him. It was unclear whether the Royal Navy let Neville keep his title. He retired early by the standards of his rank— there were rumors that he was forced to do so as a result of multiple internal investigations, but this was never confirmed. All the papers in London indicated that he stepped down by his choosing, but anyone with knowledge of the situation knew that the decision was mutual at best. I wondered if the Royal Navy knew anything about *The Response*, or whatever was their name during those early days. Was Neville already pursuing recruits to join him even while he was still on active duty?

We crept closer to the helicopter, seeking to confirm that the *Prescott* statue was indeed what was in the crate.

"Neville looks terrible," Graham said to me with his eyes wide.

Archie Neville's 6-foot 2-inch frame used to be much more svelte, at least from what I recall from our prior encounters. He had now ballooned up to near 300 pounds. He had thick gray hair that slicked back to the nape of his neck and had grown out a bit of a beard. He was still a decent-looking guy, but it was harder to find those redeeming traits under the excess fat and hair.

"Yeah, he looks like death. Must be enjoying too much booze up there in Vermont," Graham said.

The humidity had not ceased. Even though it was close to 1 a.m., we were still dealing with difficulties trying to catch our breath. If I am going to continue doing this stuff with Graham, I would need to get into shape again.

"Stay here. I'm going to get a closer look," Graham said.

I kept my back glued to the high concrete wall as Graham made some risky maneuvers that got him even closer to *The Response*. I was losing sight of him and wishing I had the same night vision technology that the *Raiders* had available. When I had my last glimpse of Graham, he was about 50 yards away from me.

Blap, blap, blap, blap, blap

My heart jumped out of my chest.

What just happened?

I ran towards the area I last saw my partner. I'm not overly familiar with the sound of gunshots, but there sure wasn't much else that sound could have been. Just as I hit peak speed, I saw Graham running towards me. Thank God he was still alive. Somewhat ungracefully, I geared down so I could shift course to run alongside him back in the other direction.

"What're you doing, Pierce?! I told you to stay put."

We were neck and neck now heading back for the Sea Ray. I didn't have the heart to look back to see what was on our tails. I just kept my eyes forward towards the dock. Graham was going to have to fill me in later.

Blap, blap

Right when I didn't think that my adrenaline could get any higher. I could see the sand and grass fly up in the air around me as we neared the dock.

Blap

Another short burst of bullets crashed through the wood of the dock.

We hopped in the Sea Ray just in time. Graham violently maneuvered us out from the island to safety. Swerving in whatever direction would throw the *Raiders* off our trail.

Blap, blap, blap

You could see the bullets splashing up water in all directions surrounding the boat, even in the darkness. One wrong move, and Graham would steer us directly into the line of fire.

Graham took care of it. We were safe now and, on our way, back to the Navy Yard.

We didn't have the statue, but we had our lives.

Twenty-One

"Graham, are you alright?"

Graham's suit was soaking wet from sweat. He removed his jacket to find a pool of blood forming on the right side of what was once a crisp white shirt.

"It just grazed me. No damage done to anything important."

"How do you know that?"

It certainly didn't look like no damage from my perspective.

"Because believe it or not, this isn't my first time taking a bullet."

Graham pressed the wound with his left hand and continued to guide the boat with his right.

"What the hell happened?" I asked as I shook, still in shock.

"Well, they killed Carlson."

"They did what? Did they find out that he led us to their location?"

"I'm not entirely sure. It was difficult to hear everything they were saying. I only picked up bits and pieces of their conversation."

"Why else would they kill him?"

"I don't think they killed him because he brought us there, but because he didn't deliver you directly to Neville's helicopter. Or maybe because he didn't do the job he was supposed to do on the USS *Constitution*. From what I heard, Neville was hoping to bring you back to Vermont. That I know for sure, you're what he wants more than anything."

"But why?"

"I don't know. My best guess is he wants to know everything you know about the *Constitution* and whatever is hiding behind this secret panel. Pierce, I think Carlson brought us here on purpose."

I had little to say for the rest of the trip home. I just wanted to get back to Charlestown as soon as possible so we could get Graham some help. As we pulled up to the Navy Yard, we realized that our problems stemmed far beyond what we thought.

The USS *Constitution* was gone.

Twenty-Two

"Damn it!" Graham attempted to say as he winced.

I wasn't sure if it was sweat or tears streaming down his cheeks now.

The *Constitution* had disappeared somewhere into the summer night sea. History itself left the dock from Charlestown, and we were now responsible for whether it would return. What we had going in our favor was the fact that we knew who was responsible for stealing her. What was not going in our favor was how they got it out of here so quickly and where they took it. My thought is *The Response* used one of their fancy yachts to pull *Old Ironsides* away from the Navy Yard. Where they took it? I assumed they weren't taking it to George's Island to meet up with the other *Response* members holding the *Prescott* statue hostage. Otherwise, we would have noticed them passing upon our return.

There were a lot of questions that needed an answer. In the meantime, Graham was continuing to lose blood, and I could tell that his overall health was declining. We had to get him help.

We tied off *The Response*'s Sea Ray on the nearest pier. We left the boat and headed up the street towards the bookshop.

"We need to get you to a hospital, Graham."

He was in a daze at this point, but it didn't stop him from informing me that going to the hospital wasn't an option, and we surely didn't have time to get him to the FBI Field Office to figure out what they wanted the next steps to be. We only made it halfway back before I was dangling Graham off my shoulder.

Finally, we made it to the bookshop. I tried to pull Graham up the stairs, but the special agent was slipping. It was a toss-up whether we would make it up the stairwell without both of us tumbling back down.

Thud.

Graham's body dropped and fell back a few steps. The next thing I knew, Lucy was in the stairwell in her nightgown, helping me carry Graham's bloodied body up the second flight of stairs to the study where there would be room to lay him down and figure out what to do.

"We need to get a nurse! There's one next door—I met her on my walk a few days ago. I told her all about your concussion, and she gave me tips on how to care for you. I'll go get her," Lucy said.

We managed to get Graham to the study and laid him down on top of some towels in the bathtub. Neither of us knew what we were doing, but it made sense that things might get messy. Lucy started running back down the stairs to go track down the nurse she had met. I felt terrible that she was now further dragged into this. Without time to remind her not to share with the nurse why Graham was in this state, I had to trust that she would keep our cover to the best of her ability. This meant that I would need to come up with a reason why my friend was in the bathtub with gunshot wounds.

During the long fifteen minutes of Lucy's departure, I did what I could to keep Graham conscious. I was splashing him with water every minute or so, but it didn't seem to be doing much good.

Then I heard footsteps sprinting up the stairwell. I knew we were in a race against the clock. I quickly recited the Lord's prayer over Graham and made it about halfway through before the door flung open. Much to my relief, it was Lucy, accompanied by the nurse. She had pulled it off. Thanks to Lucy—Graham had a chance at making it.

The nurse got to work, not asking questions in a way to make me feel uncomfortable or blame me, but to get all of the necessary information that she needed to do her job. When did he pass out? When was he shot? How much blood did I think he'd lost? These were all questions I could handle, and after answering them, the nurse sent us out of the room so she could focus on her patient.

Lucy and I left the room and told the nurse that we would be just outside in the study's sitting quarters if she needed us. Lucy and I sat down on the couch. I looked into her eyes, and she finally broke down. Through the tears and the subtle shaking, I could still make out the message she was trying to get across to me. That message was essentially, "what in the hell is going on?" I shared some of the same concerns.

"Who shot him?" Lucy asked directly.

"*The Response* did it. *The Response* shot him."

"Did they shoot at you, too?"

Even though I knew that question was coming, I wasn't sure how to answer it, but since they had already jumped me the other night, I figured it wouldn't be too much of a shock that they wanted me dead as well.

"Yeah, but Graham was looking out for me. There was no way he was going to let one of those bullets touch me."

"You don't know that, Pierce!" Lucy shouted.

She was right. But I had to believe it if we were going to complete our mission. That's if Graham is going to be able to make it through the night.

"Is this how you want to die? At the hands of these people? What's the point?"

Of course, there was a point, and I knew that Lucy recognized it deep down, or else she wouldn't have come to Boston with me in the first place.

"I'm not going to die, Lucy."

Lucy shook her head in disgust at my lack of concern. By failing to take the dangers of what I was doing as seriously as she would prefer. There was nothing I could say at this moment to bring her much comfort as our new friend fights for his life. I just wrapped my arms around her and brought her closer to me. The month since our honeymoon had been a ride, this was probably our lowest moment so far, but oddly I was relieved to know that she was still by my side. She still felt strongly that we were in the right place. Otherwise, she would pull away, but instead, she wrapped her arms around my body and squeezed tighter.

Such a hug brought me comfort that we would make it through anything in this life. Now I just needed Graham to get through this so we could figure out some way to make sense of what was happening.

Where did we go wrong?

Where do we go from here?

Twenty-Three

Lucy was emotionally drained and soon fell asleep next to me on the couch. It had been a couple of hours since I heard anything from the nurse. It was around 4:00 a.m. now, and I finally admitted to myself that it was pointless to try to get sleep until I had more information on how Graham was recovering. Soon I planned to check on the nurse and see what kind of progress she was making, but at the same time, I didn't want to wake up Lucy if I didn't have to, and I figured no news was good news in terms of Graham's current state. So, instead of getting up, I stayed on the couch for another hour or so until I started to see the early summer dawn break through the window sills.

"Mr. Spruce," said the nurse as she exited the bathroom of the study, "oh, I'm sorry, Lucy, I didn't know you were still here. I figured you had gone to bed hours ago."

Lucy lifted her head and slightly opened her eyelids.

"How's he doing?" I asked.

"He's one tough guy. It took some time to stabilize him and rein in the bleeding, but once that was under control and I got an IV in him, he started to improve. He was right that there was no organ or other extensive damage done to his side. He just lost a lot of blood and was probably dehydrated, to begin with, given the heat. You know he should see a doctor, Mr. Spruce. I would be happy to make some calls to get him in this morning. Would you like me to do that for you?"

"Why don't we hold off on that for now? If he's awake and talking, I would like him to make that decision for himself."

"Okay, but he needs help as soon as possible. I'm serious when I say that these things can get worse if not taken care of correctly. He could have internal bleeding that we don't know about or get an infection. There are just a lot of risks that a doctor would need to rule out."

"I appreciate that. I would just feel more comfortable with him making decisions for himself if he's up for it."

"Well, it seems like he wants his boss to make the decision. Whenever he was conscious, he kept asking me for a phone to call his boss. What exactly does he do? Does it have something to do with him getting shot?"

I was hoping I would avoid these questions somehow, which was naive of me to think. After all, Lucy did just wake up this kind nurse she hardly knew in the middle of the night to see if she could save our friend who was fighting for his life from a gunshot wound. Suppose that gives her the right to know what was going on.

"He's an old friend of mine who works for the State Department in Washington, DC He was just in Boston to see the bookshop. We have no idea how we found ourselves anywhere near the situation that occurred, but I assure you it's far from what we anticipated when we went out on the boat simply to relax and have a few beers on the water. The wound was the result of a stray bullet from a shooting on a nearby dock. We weren't that close to the altercation, but we could hear the gunfire, and then Graham felt a sting in his side. It was a ricochet situation," I said.

It seemed believable enough from my perspective, and we did think Graham got hit by ricochet, so it wasn't a total lie.

"Yeah, State Department, Okay, Mr. Spruce," the nurse said—still not convinced.

I guess I needed to work on my cover a bit more.

"I'm an ER nurse in a major city. I know the line of work that victims like this are in. My guess is he's an undercover detective for the Boston Police Department—in which case I assure we are able to help without compromising confidential information relating to any ongoing investigation."

So why did she ask me then?

"Please just promise me he will see a doctor. I need to head out for my shift now. I won't bring him with me, but I do want to see him walk through the doors of my hospital at some point today," the nurse instructed.

"You got it. Thanks so much for your help. Lucy and I are so grateful that we met you and that you would do such a thing for our friend means a lot. We would love to have you over for dinner sometime in the future," I said.

"No need, I'm a nurse; this is why I do what I do. It helps get me through the 12-hour shifts. But yes, I would love to come over for dinner sometime if that's okay with you, Lucy?"

Lucy's head perked back up from my chest. "Yes, please do. We're so excited to meet more people in the neighborhood."

"Pierce, get the hell in here," Graham shouted from the tub.

"Sounds like we both have work to do, Mr. Spruce. I look forward to seeing you later today."

Lucy got up to escort her new friend down the stairs.

"Pierce. Come, help me!"

I rushed into the bathroom to find Graham attempting to stand. This was going to be a long process.

"Stay down."

"Get me that robe over there, and bring me to the couch."

"No way, you need to stay where you're at."

"I'm not staying in this damn bathtub. Get me out of here."

I gave in and helped Graham make his way into the sitting area. He was walking gingerly, of course, but part of that could be due to exhaustion and dehydration. The bullet itself didn't seem to cause any lasting damage. The unfortunate reality that we both recognized was that Graham would need to get some of his strength back in the next 24 hours, that is, if we were to have any prayer of stopping *The Response* before the end of their 4ᵗʰ of July deadline. If Graham's health didn't improve drastically by this time tomorrow, our chances of recovering *Old Ironsides* would be close to zero. I settled him on the Chesterfield sofa, and we began to put together a new plan.

"Where do you think they're taking it?" I started with the obvious question.

"I don't know, but I bet they all knew we were on George's Island the whole time. They just wanted to get us away from Charlestown so they could take off with the *Constitution*. The *Colonel Prescott* statue that *The Response* stole before we arrived was more than likely just a pawn to keep our focus off the grand prize, but I'm sure they're still thrilled to have the statue."

I could tell that it was difficult for Graham to shake the embarrassment of having one pulled over on him. Graham took his job seriously, and this wasn't a case that he wanted to have slip away from him. I felt guilty myself, considering I was the one that wanted to leave the *Constitution* to recover the *Prescott* statue in the first place.

"So, there's no way they're sailing it?" Graham asked me.

"No, they're too smart to do that. It would take entirely too long to get it away from the piers, not to mention get the whole thing rigged and do everything else required to get to top speed. Plus, not enough wind on a summer night like this. They definitely took one of their yachts and are towing it along from behind. I just don't know where they're taking it. My first thought would be back to George's Island and stowing it behind Fort Warren, but I still think we would've seen them last night if that was the case. I also think they're working off of the assumption that we're coming back for them, and the obvious place for us to start our search would be George's Island."

"We need to give the director a call and let him know the latest before we do anything drastic. He'll be angry, but he'll get over that quickly because he knows we need his guidance, not his frustration."

"Who is going to dial-up the director?" I asked with my fingers crossed it wouldn't have to be me.

"I think you should do it, Pierce. He's going to be a whole lot more understanding with his godson than he is with his special agent right now."

"Fine," I said as I uncrossed my fingers.

No part of me wanted to be the one to give the director the news that not only had we not recovered the *Prescott* statue, but we'd also managed to give up one of America's most famous battleships in the process.

My uncrossed fingers were now slowly dialing the director's direct line.

He picked up after one ring.

"Hello?"

"Mr. Director, it's Pierce. We have bad news."

"Okay," the director responded somberly.

"*The Response* is now in possession of the USS *Constitution*. They led us on to the whereabouts of the *Colonel Prescott* statue on purpose to pull us away from the Navy Yard."

"I see. Where are you now?"

"Back in Charlestown. Special Agent Graham was hit on his side by a *Response* bullet. A nurse came to the bookshop and confirmed that there's no reason to have any concerns. She does want him to go see a doctor, but he's not planning to do so."

"Put him on the phone."

I looked at Graham, gave him a nod, and pointed at the phone to indicate that the director wanted to speak with him. He shook his head no. I couldn't say I blamed him. Talking to his boss was probably the last thing he needed right now.

"Graham is asleep, Mr. Director. Should I wake him up?"

"No, that's fine. He probably needs the rest. Have him give me a call when he wakes up."

"Will do, sir."

"The two of you better re-assess things and come up with a better plan than you have thus far. This country needs its history. I'm trusting you both to recover these pieces of it before it's too late."

"I know, sir. I know. We'll come up with a new strategy."

"Get some rest, Pierce. Take care of yourself."

"You too, sir."

I hung up the phone and started to tell Graham that the director wanted an update from us later on that morning, but Graham wasn't listening to me. He was sound asleep, and my own eyelids could barely be kept open. It was about 5:30 a.m. now. I headed down to the second floor to join Lucy in bed. After a quick cold shower to rinse the dirt and blood off of my body—I was finally able to settle into bed.

I feared I wouldn't be able to sleep given how upset and worried I was, but once I got in the covers and wrapped my body around Lucy—I settled down.

My eyes closed, and I put my concerns on hold for a few hours.

Twenty-Four

Beep-Beep-Beep...Slam!

I hit the alarm clock. It doesn't even feel like I fell asleep. *Did the alarm go off early?* When I looked over at the clock, I saw the unfortunate reality that it truly was 9:00 a.m., the exact time I set it for. One day I would need to catch up on all of the sleep I was missing out on. Lucy was already out of bed. The sheets were neatly tucked back in on her side. I stared at the ceiling for about five minutes with my hands interlocked behind my head. Before I got too deep into thought, Lucy opened the door and brought in a fresh cup of coffee.

"I thought I heard you wake up. How'd you sleep?" Lucy asked as she handed me the mug.

I took a sip, a small one due to the heat, before responding.

"Not great—it certainly doesn't feel like 9:00 a.m. already."

"I went up to check on Graham about half an hour ago. He's still sound asleep, but his color looks a lot better than it did last night or earlier this morning, I guess. I put a glass of water next to the couch for when he wakes up. Do you think it's worth waking him up so we can move him to his bed?"

"Thank you for doing that, honey. I wouldn't worry about moving him to his bed. He probably has no idea where he's sleeping. Let's just let him wake up when he wakes up and figure it out from there."

"Okay, I feel more comfortable leaving him now that he's starting to look better. Are you going to take him to the hospital today?"

"No, unfortunately, we can't do that. The doctors would need answers to questions that we can't provide them."

Lucy took a sip of her coffee. I could see her brows raise and eyes roll as she lifted the mug to her lips. She didn't ask again, but I could tell that she thought we were crazy for not bringing a man who just got shot to the hospital. Typically, in another circumstance, I would be on Lucy's side—now I just hoped that the FBI would send someone to the bookshop to look at Graham and ensure he was good to go. Even if that doesn't happen, I knew that Graham would be ready once he woke up, showered, and got some coffee in him. He was a Marine, after all.

"What're you going to do until he wakes up?"

"I'm not sure. I probably can't open the bookshop today just in case things go south with Graham or the fact that our timeline for putting an end to *The Response* got so accelerated last night. I know we didn't get the chance to go through all of the details that happened last night, Lucy. To be honest, it's all blurry to me as well, but what we know for sure is that when we took off for George's Island, the USS *Constitution* was still safely stationed in the Navy Yard, and when we returned from the island, it wasn't."

"Where do you think they took it to?"

"I have no idea. Would you like to take a walk to the Navy Yard with me to check it out? We didn't have time to get a good look at it last night—given Graham's condition."

"Yes. I would love that. That is if you think it would be helpful."

Lucy got dressed, and we walked our usual route to the Navy Yard. You could tell that many civilians taking their morning stroll were confused to see that the iconic ship wasn't in its usual location. I could already hear murmurs of questions.

Where was it? What happened to the USS *Constitution?*

I was going to start telling the people walking by that the *Constitution* was undergoing restorations and that it had to go to another naval base for repairs or something along those lines. I thought twice about that approach, as it may have led to more questions. The worst of which would be how I knew that the ship was out for repairs and why they couldn't just do them here in the Navy Yard. I could only hope that the director would be talking to the mayor as soon as possible about what the cover story was going to be. That is if they would even be willing to tell the mayor anything close to the truth.

Lucy and I traced the pier for any signs of the heist. There was nothing of note at the scene that would be helpful to us. But then again, what did I know about investigating a crime scene? The one potential saving grace that hadn't occurred to me until I was back on the pier was the small cameras that Graham had placed on and around the *Constitution*.

"Let's continue our walk. There's nothing to see here. It will be back to the drawing board for Graham and me. Now, I just prayed that the cameras were able to catch something that may lead us in the right direction."

"I just don't understand how they moved it so quickly without anyone noticing?"

"We don't know whether or not anyone noticed. That's why we need to look at the security cameras. Maybe there was someone around when it happened. Someone we could find in Charlestown, but that still wouldn't answer the question of where they were taking it."

"I guess you'll find out where they took it soon enough. So, is there anything else you want to check out, or should we just turn around and head home? I want to get back within the hour so I can make sure Graham has everything he needs."

"You're so good to him."

"He was shot last night, Pierce. Plus, he's practically becoming family. I mean, he does live with us."

She was right, Graham was quickly becoming part of our family. Although, I hoped we wouldn't need to be working together forever. I wasn't sure how long I could make it as a pseudo volunteer agent. I wasn't doing a great job so far.

"Pierce, I'm sorry about what happened last night. Are you at all scared of what might come next?"

"Yeah, but not for my safety. I fear for Graham, as strong as he is, that my lack of experience might get him killed. I'm scared that we won't recover the *William Prescott* statue or the USS *Constitution*, not to mention my father's JFK manuscript. Not much has gone as planned since Graham and I started working together. It's hard to tell if that's because we don't have the right strategy in place, or if *The Response* is just that skilled, probably a little bit of both. Where we go from here, I don't know. The director brought me here to stop *The Response* from doing further damage. Since my arrival, they've only increased their number of successful heists. The expectation was that we would, at worst, protect the USS *Constitution*, and at best, recover the stolen statue. I've failed to do either."

"Don't do this to yourself, Pierce. If the director didn't have faith in you, then he wouldn't have brought you to Boston in the first place. If he thought Graham needed the assistance of a great special agent, then he would have had plenty of people to choose from to be by Graham's side. He chose you because you have a different skill set. I think he knew there was a good possibility that you and Graham would struggle at the start. You're vastly outnumbered, after all. Maybe he chose you not just for your brain, your connections, or your resources, but because he knew you wouldn't back down once the operation became challenging."

"I just fear it may go on for a while. *The Response* has what sounds like hundreds of members now, and they seem to be growing."

"Exactly. You and Graham versus hundreds. Let's say this does go on for a while, and you're just getting started, then maybe you and Graham need to learn to trust each other even more. Play to each other's strengths and learn each other's weaknesses because I agree—if you refuse to change—then you'll both be at a high risk of not making it home. And you better always make it home, Pierce. If this mission is as important to you as it seems—then I am willing to support you. But if things escalate much further without improvement—I am afraid my need for you to be safe will soon outweigh everything else."

That put things back into perspective. Lucy and I hadn't even had that much time to talk the past month. I would've never guessed that she was so invested in our success with this operation. Her commitment to the cause reminded me not just why I loved her but also why it's so crucial that Graham and I succeed.

"Understood," I confirmed.

What else could I say? She had laid out her terms. It was up to Graham and me to deliver.

We made our way back past the rows of townhouses and brick walk-ups. Most were waving navy flags that had a green tree in the upper corner. The flag of Bunker Hill.

We took the short route home, so it only took about ten minutes before we walked through the bookshop's front door.

It was time to wake up FBI Special Agent Robert Graham.

We had a lot to discuss.

Twenty-Five

"Wake up, Graham. Graham, wake up. It's time for lunch."

I brought Graham a sandwich and left it on the coffee table next to the couch. His eyes slowly opened.

"My head is pounding. How much blood did I lose?"

"The nurse said you lost quite a bit, but she didn't take you to the hospital, so you must still have enough in the tank to survive."

"Easy for you to say. Feels like I got run over by a train," Graham said as he lifted his body into a seated position and started to pick at his sandwich.

"Aren't you hungry?"

"Yes and no. I would love to scarf this down right now, but it hurts when my ribs move. I must've broken one. Whatever, we don't have time to worry about me. I hope I was hallucinating last night about the *Constitution* being gone."

"You weren't. *The Response* took it. Lucy and I walked through the Navy Yard this morning to confirm. I thought you and I could take a look at the surveillance tapes to see if we can come up with any leads.

Nothing that I saw at the pier eluded to where they may have taken it."

"Alright, let's see what we can find," Graham said as he brought his sandwich over to the section of the study that we had been referring to as the "Command Center." There were three monitors set up that rotated views of the bookshop, the *Constitution* itself, and the area surrounding it. Rather, the area that used to surround it.

"They must've been smart enough to check the ship for cameras because they broke the ones that were on it. We still have a visual from the cameras that we placed on the pier, though. Those confirm that two *Response Raiders* were on the *Constitution*, and as you suspected, one other *Raider* is out in front steering one of their yachts. The two *Raiders* in the back hooked the *Constitution's* front to the yacht and took off. Crazy how easy it was for them. It doesn't even look like any civilians were around to see it happen. This section of the tape was only about ten minutes long. That's a pretty quick heist on their part—very few errors and no real trail left behind. They just got in and got out," Graham said.

It's scary to think that stealing such an iconic piece of history could happen in less than ten minutes. Of course, museums could contain their artifacts via heightened internal security systems. But, being outside in the open, no matter how much protection was in place to monitor the *Constitution*, it was hard to imagine how you would stop highly trained operatives from taking the vessel if they wanted it badly enough.

"Pierce, I need your help here. This video recording from the cameras is going to give us nothing. Where do you think they would bring the *Constitution*?"

If I knew for sure, we would already be on our way to that location, but I knew that wouldn't be a good enough answer for Graham. I ran my hands through my hair that I had not had the chance to get trimmed since before the wedding. Soon enough, I may be pulling it out myself. I continued to look at the bookshelves. So far, no book had the answer to this one. I had read about the *Constitution*, but what I needed at this point was a book about *The Response*. But at the same time, I needed such a book—I prayed that one would never be written.

I never wanted anyone to learn about *The Response*'s existence.

I sighed and took a bite of my sandwich. Graham was aimlessly fiddling with his pen and legal pad, as he had quickly given up on the security recordings.

"Graham, I know I said that I would take the *Constitution* to Europe, but even with the yacht dragging it, I don't think they could make it there fast enough without getting caught. And we know they won't be able to get it delivered to Neville's landlocked cabin. That would take far too much time to have it shipped in a truck or something. They would need to break *Old Ironsides* down to its basic parts if they were going to do that."

"They might be crazy enough to do that, Pierce. I wouldn't put it past them."

Graham had a point. There's probably no limit with Archie Neville anymore. He'll do whatever it takes to get what he wants.

"I don't think he'll cut it up. I know he's ruthless, but I don't think cutting it up would serve his purpose without knowing exactly where the hidden panel is."

"That's a good point," Graham confirmed.

We sat in silence for a moment.

"Graham, how are you feeling? Are you up to go back to George's Island this afternoon? There might be something there that was left behind last night either by them or us that could help in our search."

Graham's face grimaced as he pushed off the arms of his chair and started to rise to his feet.

"Yeah, let's do that," Graham attempted to say as his teeth clenched, and he buttoned up his shirt.

"You sure? I can go alone if I need to."

"And what're you going to do if the *Raiders* are still there?"

"My assumption is that there'll be far too many civilians there at this time of day. *The Response* would be wise to be long gone by now."

"Either way, you need back up. Even if I can't move, I still have a better chance of protecting you than you do of protecting yourself."

"I guess I can't argue with that. You know, Graham, I wouldn't be offended if you didn't wear a suit. That can't be comfortable right now."

Graham continued to get dressed—completing his half Windsor knot to the best of his current ability.

"Are you kidding me, Pierce? Consider this my armor."

Unfortunately, this particular armor wasn't capable of stopping bullets. He was crazy for wanting to wear a suit in the first place, it was close to 90 degrees and as humid as it could get, but he was too hard-headed to let that phase him—which I could appreciate.

"Doesn't the Bureau give you some kind of bulletproof vest when you become an agent?"

"I could complain all day about how uncomfortable those things are—I can barely move in mine when it's outside of my suit. I'll probably start wearing one now, though—I'm going to get you one too."

"I would greatly appreciate that. I guess I can't speak to the discomfort of wearing a bulletproof vest—just don't complain to me about being hot in that suit. I gave you an out."

"Come on, enough about my wardrobe. Let's take the Sea Ray out for another joy ride."

I was getting used to my walk to the Navy Yard. Graham was moving very gingerly. It took twice as long to get to the pier where we left the Sea Ray as it had last night, but he did appear to be moving a little better with each step. As painful as it seemed to be for him to walk—you could tell that his confidence was coming back as his stride slowly made its way back to normalcy. Plus, I didn't need him for his walking ability as much as his seamanship. Once we were on the boat, he moved a little quicker—getting us out on the water in short order.

We were on our way back to the scene of last night's shooting. I wondered if any tourists had a clue about the action that took place at Fort Warren less than 24 hours ago.

Would we show up to a fort covered with yellow caution tape? What kind of blood trail did we leave behind? What did The Response leave behind?

We could hope for evidence of their presence, but I wasn't optimistic. That would be a beginner's mistake on their part, and they were far from beginners.

A few weeks ago, Graham and I wanted nothing more than the

chance to meet *The Response* face to face. Now that that encounter had occurred on multiple violent occasions—we needed to have a bit more respect for our adversary.

The Response was ready for a fight to the death.

The question was—were we? And where was that fight going to take place if we were?

Twenty-Six

I was a bit surprised about what I saw as we approached the dock at Fort Warren. Less than twelve hours ago, there were no other boats in sight, now the dock was full of boats and ferries transporting patrons in and out. It was a typical summer day at such a tourist attraction in Boston. Especially the day before the 4th of July, it wasn't an uncommon time of year to see so many retirees, young families, and camp trips making their way to visit the old Civil War prison. What struck me as odd was what we found as we walked back past the northern wall, the shipping container from last night—it was still there.

"What? Graham is that the container?" My voice raised as I pointed in shock. "You think the statue is still in there?"

I looked back in Graham's direction—he was trailing far from behind. I was probably walking too fast for his mangled condition. He was breathing heavily in my wake.

I couldn't imagine they would risk so much to steal the statue in the first place just to give it right back. Especially now that they knew they had us outmatched.

"I'm sure they moved it. Maybe they put it back on the yacht and moved it to wherever they're bringing the *Constitution* until they find a way to get it to Neville's cabin. Only one way to find out," Graham said as he finally walked past me—making his way towards the storage container.

"Can we do this in front of all these people?"

It seemed odd that none of the tourists would ask one of the guides what was in the container or that the guides or security hadn't questioned the container's existence in the first place. I guess everyone assumed that someone else was taking care of it, which means no one would take care of it.

"No tourists should be coming this way. They're all inside the fort," Graham said.

A few people were lingering outside the fort, but I guess Graham was right. No one seemed to question the container's existence yet, so if we went over to check it out, no one would think twice about it.

"Right behind you," I said as I jogged five yards to catch up.

We made our way to the front of the container. No one even locked it. Graham opened the door, and I held my breath.

"There it is," Graham said with a sigh of relief. "Fully intact, too. It doesn't look like there's a scratch on him."

I was equally relieved but also wary. The fact that they risked so much to obtain the *Prescott* statue as a ploy to get what they wanted proved that *The Response* had no regard for anything.

"We'll just need to call it in to the director. He'll know how to diplomatically return the statue without telling anyone at the Bureau what the statue is doing at Fort Warren. We can say it was moved for a commemorative event or something. The people sent to recover it probably won't even know where the statue's proper home is until they bring it back to Bunker Hill for us and see the vacant platform."

"That makes sense. I mean—we definitely can't move it ourselves."

"Let's keep looking around to see if we can find anything else. When we get back to the boat, I'll let the director know that he should send a recovery team for the statue."

We kept looking around, but anything left from the firefight last night had been washed away or cleaned by the *Raiders*. They left nothing. There was no evidence of their existence.

"I will give them credit for one thing. They know what they're doing," Graham said as he continued to search the area where they killed Conan Carlson. We had no clue what they did with the body, but it too had disappeared. Presumably, *The Response* threw him in the water.

We spent a solid 30 minutes searching for answers but came up with nothing. Wherever *The Response* was going next—Fort Warren didn't hold the answer.

We hopped back on the Sea Ray that formerly belonged to Carlson and *The Response* and made our way back to Charlestown. Graham decided to wait until we were back in the study to call the director. It was clear that the *Prescott* statue was of little value to *The Response* at the moment, and no risk remained in having it sit at Fort Warren until the FBI could bring it safely back.

"Are you surprised they left the statue?" I asked.

"I am—and I'm not. Nothing surprises me anymore. I've been doing this job long enough to know that you can never assume what the enemy will do next. Each case is new. You can do your best to rely on your experience, but you have to think outside the box and never get too comfortable when all is said and done. The criminals I go up against are wanted for a reason, and that reason is they pose a real threat. The people I deal with don't stick to patterns. They always keep you guessing. They hope you sit on your heels long enough to allow them to execute whatever grand scheme they have in mind next. In this case, that grand scheme was the *Constitution*, but that doesn't mean we acted inappropriately by chasing down the statue. We decided to act on the information we knew. You can kill yourself overthinking what you should've done in hindsight doing this job, but we can't let ourselves fall victim to that."

"That's why I'm glad I have you, so I don't have to worry about the discipline it takes to be a good special agent. I can continue being as naive as I want and thinking the best of people," I said.

"Those feelings will go away soon enough. You just wait. There are more Archie Neville's in the world than anyone would like to know."

157

"I hope they don't all want to kill me."

"No. I think it's just him that wants to kill you, but as I said, nothing surprises me, so maybe you're on a few lists," Graham said with a chuckle.

"Well, if they do get me, I blame you."

"Fine. I'm not going to let you die, though."

"Because you need my help?"

"No, because I know Lucy would be upset, and I don't want to do that to her."

"Thanks, Graham. I'm sure Lucy appreciates it."

We arrived at the Navy Yard and made the familiar walk from the piers to the bookshop.

"Another day is going by with the bookshop being closed. Lucy might be right about the bookshop going bankrupt before this operation is complete," I said.

"She said what?" Graham responded in shock.

"She said I'm running the bookshop into the ground."

"That's hilarious. Did you tell her you're a bit preoccupied? And a billionaire?"

"It wasn't a battle that I wanted to fight."

We arrived back at the currently closed bookshop and walked up to the study. It was time to get back to the drawing board.

Graham called up the director. I could hear him requesting that a group of agents who could be trusted pick up the statue. After that, all I heard was Graham updating the director about how he was feeling. Graham was so active at Fort Warren that I had almost forgotten he was fighting a lot of pain even to be standing. Once the director had all the current information and knew where the FBI could pick up the statue, the focus shifted to the *Constitution*. They chatted for a few more minutes before Graham hung up and joined me back in the study's main sitting area.

"The director didn't have any good advice for us. Just told us to figure it out and try not to get shot."

"I agree with him."

"You and I both. Do you have any insights from all of your research books?"

"I've tried and tried to find the answers from them. The books about the *Constitution* have taken me a long way, but I don't think they can tell us what we need to do next. I've begun to map out a few ideas on this legal pad."

"Show me what you've come up with so far."

"Well, we know they can't get the *Constitution* too far away from Boston. And at this point my assumption is they will either leave the ship altogether or destroy it once they have figured out what's behind the panel, if anything."

"That's interesting," Graham said as he rubbed his temples for an extended period. He was clenching his teeth again like earlier. It was becoming difficult to tell whether it was due to his physical pain or the mental agony he was putting on himself trying to play chess with *The Response.*

"Graham, why don't you go lay down and rest. I can keep backtracking and trying to figure out a few options where *The Response* could reasonably hide the *Constitution* without anyone seeing her. Once I have an idea of the location, I'll need you at full strength to act."

"You sure, Pierce? I'm willing to battle through, but to be honest, my head is pounding."

"Absolutely. Get a few hours of sleep. We can go over what I come up with tonight after dinner. We would only be wasting our time if we went out looking for the *Constitution* right now. I wouldn't know where to begin to look—this isn't a situation where the guess and check method is going to help matters."

"Thanks, Pierce. Let's meet back in the study around 7:00 tonight. An afternoon of rest should get my body reacclimated to its normal state, or at least close enough."

"My thoughts exactly—go rest up."

It was five hours until we planned to meet back up. Hopefully, it would be enough time for me to dig deep into everything I knew about the USS *Constitution* and *The Response* in order to crack the code of where both were currently.

But first, I was going to need a fresh pot of coffee.

Twenty-Seven

With a mug of coffee in hand, I sat down at the desk and got back to work. I stared at my notes. I was circling and underlining some of the thoughts I had laid out for Graham.

The top of my legal pad had the following three points.

- The location will need to be close to New England.
- They want to find the "secret panel" inside the captain's cabin of the USS *Constitution* (plan to destroy it by sunset on the 4th of July if deemed necessary).
- Want to get rid of me.

As I stared at my notes, I tried to reflect on my knowledge of New England and what kind of location *The Response* would be able to take the *Constitution* that would accomplish all of these goals. In my mind, *The Response* had limited time to do anything with the *Constitution* because the longer it was in motion—the greater the chance of someone recognizing the vessel. It's not like they could just dock the *Constitution* anywhere without garnering some semblance of attention. I felt like I needed to focus my efforts on the three most likely locations outside of

Boston that one might hide a large historic ship. I jotted down some additional points.

- Nova Scotia, Canada
- Cape Cod, Massachusetts
- Newport, Rhode Island

These were what I believed to be the most likely locations. Nova Scotia would make sense if they wanted to hold the *Constitution* at an island that would result in the least amount of exposure to onlookers and tourists. Cape Cod would be the most accessible location to get to if you were factoring in distance alone.

But after taking a critical look at these options, and given *The Response's* priorities that we were currently aware of, it seemed that Newport, Rhode Island, was the most likely of the listed destinations. If for no other reason than the fact that they had been there recently to steal books from The Naval War College. I assume this meant that *The Response* had more back-up in Newport than they would in Nova Scotia or Cape Cod. Plus, Newport was close enough to get to within the darkest point of the night, so *The Response Raiders* would have been able to arrive and dock before dawn. Giving them a better chance of avoiding being spotted.

And, of course, it was the location where Archie Neville had my parents killed. So, I'm sure he would enjoy nothing more than killing me, the only remaining member of my family, in that same location. But only after I give him whatever "secret information" he thinks I have.

I circled *Newport, Rhode Island*, on the page, but I wanted to get Graham's input before I fully committed to that being the place we should take a chance on. We had such limited time that we couldn't afford to be wrong. Otherwise, it would be too late. Tomorrow was the 4th of July, so we assumed, based on what Morgan told Carlson about *The Response's* "Plan B," that Neville was going to do everything in his power to do something with the USS *Constitution* by the end of the day tomorrow.

My only hesitation with Newport was where they would keep the

Constitution. There were plenty of places to dock a boat in Newport, but would any of those locations allow *The Response* to hide until they were ready to execute whatever plan they had in mind as the *Constitution's* fate? That was a question that I didn't know the answer to but would need to figure out. My other concern with Newport was whether I was putting too much focus on myself. Was I putting more emphasis on Newport because that's where my parents died?

I spent the next few hours reading more about The Naval War College to see what kind of additional information I could gather and if there were any ties between it and the USS *Constitution.*

After finalizing my notes, I headed downstairs to enjoy some dinner with Lucy before I needed to meet back up with Graham. We took our time with the meal. I shared some of my thoughts with her, knowing I could greatly benefit from her insights. Explaining to her why I thought *The Response* would choose Newport over other locations. Lucy provided me with some constructive feedback. She mentioned that, in her opinion, Nova Scotia probably made the most sense because it was more remote, and the *Constitution* would presumably garner less attention there. Giving them more time to find a way to hide the ship permanently in a place of Neville's choosing, which we all agreed was *The Response's* preferred outcome if possible.

"Whichever place your gut is telling you to go with, I'm sure it's the right one," Lucy said before kissing my forehead.

After I rinsed off my dishes, I went back up to the study. Graham arrived right on time, his complexion looking much better than the ghostly appearance he had earlier in the day.

We kicked things off with me handing over my notepad. No words were said to begin with until Graham broke the silence.

"This is great work, Pierce."

"Do you think that I'm being objective enough, though, Graham? Newport worries me. Please tell me if you think I circled Newport solely because of what happened to my parents there."

"Not at all. The Naval War College connection makes a lot of sense. We know they've been in that area recently and, for all we know, could have been scoping out locations to hide the USS *Constitution*, and they could realistically find one of the many places to dock that would be out of sight at least for a day. Plus, even if a local sees the *Constitution* out on the water, they may not have the courage to speak up. They'll see it and say to themselves, "that looks like the USS *Constitution*," and then keep that thought to themselves. Unfortunately for us, I can't imagine more than half of local residents would even be able to tell the difference between the *Constitution* and any other large sailboat."

I wasn't sure if that was supposed to be reassuring or not.

"Are there any other locations you had in mind, Graham? I'm worried that I haven't covered every option in my notes."

"We don't have time to cover every option, Pierce. This is the best one we have, and given that we need to find *The Response* quickly, within the next 24 hours assuming they will do something with it during the 4th of July excitement tomorrow—we need to try Newport—and we need to do so now. We'll never have all the answers. It's just part of this business. So, are you ready to go?"

"Now?!"

"Yep, now. We'll need to take a car. I'll have the local field office send one over. Should be here in 15 minutes or so."

"Why don't we just take the Sea Ray?"

"I'm worried they may be having it tracked."

I hadn't thought of that, but it was a valid point.

"Yeah, car works for me. I can be ready in five."

I wasn't expecting to leave tonight. I knew we were in a race against the clock, but I assumed we wouldn't leave until the following morning. I guess nothing should surprise me working with Graham anymore.

I quickly hopped back down to the second level to slip on my "outdoor" loafers. After kissing Lucy goodbye—I met Graham down in the bookshop.

Moments later, a brown 1980 Ford Thunderbird rolled up to the front.

"That's ours. Let's go," Graham said as he led the way out the door.

He traded keys with the man driving who presumably worked for the Bureau—handing him in return the keys to the Sea Ray as we jumped in the Thunderbird. Neither said a word, which was odd that the agent dropping off the car wouldn't want to know more about the reason for the exchange. Guess they get used to not asking questions.

"Why did you give him the keys to the Sea Ray?"

Graham looked over at me and bluntly answered, "If it's under GPS surveillance. *The Response* will be thrown off because that agent is going to take the Sea Ray to Cape Cod."

That made me cringe because if my gut was wrong and *The Response* was actually at the Cape and not Newport, then I practically just hung that agent out to dry with no warning. It was clear to me at this point that any additional personnel the director sent—were in no way briefed on our mission or the risk beforehand.

Graham fired up the Thunderbird and took off.

Almost immediately, my stomach began to knot, and sweat ran across my forehead. Soon we would be on the same road my parents were on that dreadful evening.

Twenty-Eight

Newport is not far from Boston. We were lucky to have missed the holiday traffic, which allowed us to make it to Newport in short order. It's a beautiful drive, even at this time of night. Especially once you enter Newport and wind through the tree-lined roads to the mansions on the "Cliff Walk." One of these mansions was where Graham and I would be staying for the night or as long as it took to get the job done.

We arrived at the front gates of *The Breakers House*. Although *The Breakers* is a historical site now, I was still able to call in a favor to some old family friends who used to own it. The Vanderbilt's were graciously willing to let Graham and I stay at *The Breakers* so long as it was okay with the preservation society. The preservation society was happy to oblige—and for their hospitality, I promised a healthy financial donation to cover repairs for a handful of the historic mansions on the Cliff Walk.

The Breakers is a Renaissance-style mansion with beautiful limestone on the outside and an interior consisting of about 70 rooms. The estate sits on top of a rocky cliff that peers over the Atlantic Ocean. It's truly one of the most magnificent places on earth. After all these years, returning to it felt like a dream, or more so like I was traveling back in time. If only my grandparents were here to see it now. Unfortunately, there wouldn't be much time to enjoy the house given all of the work to be done. After my donation, I could only hope that they would allow me to come back sometime, hopefully with Lucy instead of Graham. We nearly had to leave again as soon as we arrived. The only thing we had time to do was drop off our bags inside the front door and hop back into our year-old Ford Thunderbird, which was now en route to The Naval War College.

The Naval War College is just over four miles away from *The Breakers*. We could see the War College's main buildings and had a pretty good view of the surrounding area. Newport seems to be the ideal location for such an institution as The Naval War College to be located. A special place where its students can stare out at the water between hours of lectures. Unfortunately, Newport is also a great location to hide a ship. At first blush, it would be hard for even us to identify the USS *Constitution* amongst all the other vessels. Assuming, of course, the *Constitution* was actually here.

We started to head north from The Naval War College, passing the Naval Academy Preparatory School and continuing past the U.S. Undersea Warfare Center. Sure, it made me wish that we could ask these well-educated military personnel for some help, but that was a fight we gave up weeks ago. We kept going until we could get some good views of Hog Island, the first location we thought *The Response* might dock. We assumed that they would want to be close enough to The Naval War College to quickly move the *Constitution* closer whenever the coast was clear. We looped around the harbor so we could get a view of the island from all angles.

Nothing.

There were a few boats off of the island, but none of them was the one we were after. We U-turned and worked our way back south. We were going to focus on the islands within our view from the road before we worried about jumping from one island to another. This would be a big commitment, given that time was a luxury we lacked at this point.

"You see anything, Pierce?" Graham asked from the driver's seat.

"Nope. Drive a little slower—that might help."

"Why? Don't you know what the USS *Constitution* looks like? An expert like yourself should only need to catch a glimpse."

"That doesn't prevent me from getting car sick in your Thunderbird, Graham."

"The Bureau can pick up the tab for any cleanup required. It would be the least they could do for us at this point."

"Right. I'm sure they would pick up the tab—since they're so gracious with their financial resources these days."

We both laughed.

"Do they drive a lot of Thunderbirds in London?"

"I couldn't tell you. I walk everywhere in London. I try to avoid looking at the roads too much."

"No wonder I'm always the one who has to drive."

"You're an FBI agent. They train you to be a good driver, don't they?" I said as Graham continued to speed down the nearly empty roads.

Still nothing.

We passed The Naval War College again and headed in the opposite direction—now going south on the coastline. I was discouraged, but I still had some hope that *The Response* was somewhere close. Even if they were in Newport, though, pinpointing their exact location would be difficult. It wasn't just time that was working against us—it was also daylight. We arrived in Newport after the sun went down, which led to me switching back and forth between regular binoculars and ones with night vision. Night vision that wasn't nearly as advanced as what *The Response Raiders* had available to them. In the ideal world, we would have waited to start our search the following day, but at that point, *Old Ironsides* may be at the bottom of the Atlantic. Who knew what *The Response* would do with the USS *Constitution* once they were done with it. We hardly understood why they wanted it in the first place. And I still couldn't recollect my father or grandfather ever discussing anything regarding a secret panel inside the ship. Nonetheless, what that panel was protecting. None of it made sense.

Once far enough south, we had the option to cut west and enter Goat Island.

We spent about an hour scouring the perimeter of the island.

Nothing. Nothing. Nothing.

We were about to head back to the mainland and keep going to the southernmost point, but Graham had another plan in mind.

"We need to get out on the water, Pierce," Graham said as he aimlessly drove around the island at about 15 miles an hour.

"How are we going to get a boat?"

"We're going to need to "borrow" one for the evening. I'm sure the owner won't mind if their boat is responsible for saving the USS *Constitution*."

"Do you know how to hotwire boats?" I asked.

"Of course!" Graham answered emphatically.

"Oh yeah, I forgot who I was talking to for a minute."

"The Bureau didn't teach me how to do it. I learned that skill on my own. I wasn't always the best kid growing up."

I couldn't help but roll my eyes. We found the nearest dock and parked the Thunderbird.

"Which one do you think we should take?" I asked.

It wasn't in my nature to steal anything, even for a good cause, but I guess Graham was right in this case. Plus, I could always replace the boat for the owner if we were to damage it. I just had to hope that it didn't hold too much sentimental value. If it were my boat, I would want the FBI to feel free to "borrow it," which was the only way to justify Graham's plan.

"How about this one? It's the same Sea Ray model as the one we took from *The Response*." Graham said from about 20 yards down the dock.

Oh yeah, I had forgotten that I already had one stolen boat on my record. What was the harm in adding another?

"Yep, that works for me, Graham. Whichever one you think you can get moving the fastest."

Graham started messing with wires. I didn't even want to pretend like I could assist him. I had no idea how boats worked. I only relaxed on deck when I was on them. It was quickly becoming apparent that my sheltered childhood had some downsides.

Vrooom...Vrooom...

The motor kicked on.

"Looks like I still got it, Pierce! Where do we want to look first?" Graham asked.

There was a map on board. But I knew from memory that we were close to another island with much less civilian activity than the ones we had been searching so far.

"There's an old lighthouse over there, on Rose Island. Let's go over there. I can't imagine many tourists would be around there at this time of night."

Graham headed for the old lighthouse. Once he could see it for himself without the binoculars, he couldn't believe such a place existed.

"That's a lighthouse? That isn't like any lighthouse I've seen—more like *The Breakers* version of a lighthouse. That's bigger than my childhood home."

"Yeah, it is indeed a lighthouse, pretty nice, huh?"

You could see an illuminated American flag flapping in the wind next to the lookout tower that rose far above the living quarters, which stood on top of a beautiful rock platform.

As we wrapped around the edge of the island where the lighthouse was, we refocused our attention ahead. It was too dark to see clearly, but on the northern tip of the island, you could make out three tall masts. Those masts could only belong to one vessel. We looked at each other and nodded in agreement without saying a word—confirming that we had found our target.

"SOMETHING! That has to be it," I said as I pulled the night vision binoculars away from my face.

"Definitely. I'm going to pull back."

"Wait, why would you do that? That's her. That's the USS *Constitution*. We've got it, Graham."

"No, we don't have it, Pierce. We're a long way from having it. We simply know where it is."

Graham whipped the Sea Ray around and went back to where we

169

came from off of Goat Island.

"Pierce, you were spot on, great work."

"Thanks, Graham. But if we don't go after them now, won't we miss our window of stopping them before the 4th?"

"If we go after them now, we not only blow our cover, we run the risk of being in an even worse spot than we were in at Fort Warren."

Graham was thinking a few steps ahead, which I appreciated since it probably saved my life. We had been incorrect about our assumptions in the past regarding the number of *Response* members in Boston. We had no idea just how many *Response Raiders* were on the USS *Constitution*, and we weren't going to be able to get close enough to get clarity without drawing attention to ourselves.

We made it back to the dock and left the Sea Ray, where we found it. No worse for the wear.

"Let's get back in the car and go back to The Naval War College."

"What are we going back to The Naval War College for?"

"I need to borrow some stuff from them."

"What kind of stuff?"

"Scuba suits."

"For who?"

"Us."

"Wait a minute, Graham. What's your plan here?"

"Haven't you scuba-dived before? I thought all rich people knew how to scuba dive."

"Yeah, actually I have, with my mom in the Caribbean, but I don't think scuba diving has anything to do with socioeconomic status, Graham."

"So how did your mom get you out there if you're so scared to do it now?"

"My father had business in Jamaica one winter, and my mom and I spent a few weeks taking lessons. I spent the first week of the trip reading by the hotel pool, but she told me I needed to broaden my horizons. I have fond memories of that trip, but it was many years ago. I haven't scuba dived since—or even thought about it for that matter."

"See, I won't have to teach you," Graham said before laughing.

"When did you learn how to scuba dive?"

"Special operation. Still classified, that's all you get to know. Are you up for it then? I'm sure The Naval War College can hook us up with what we need."

"What? I just told you I barely have any experience."

"You have almost the same amount of experience as a scuba diver as you do being an FBI agent, and you aren't terrible at that. Don't worry. We won't do anything crazy. Plus, it's not like I'm some pro scuba diver. We're in the same boat here, well we're in the car now, but you catch my drift."

With such limited options to overtake the USS *Constitution*, I guess I needed to jump on board with whatever plan gave us the best chance to succeed. With that said, I had no idea what the plan was or if there even was a plan at this point.

Regardless, there was no time to overthink things now.

Twenty-Nine

By the time our car pulled into some miscellaneous parking lot near The Naval War College, it was close to 1 a.m., and understandably no one was on standby waiting to give Graham and me some "extra scuba equipment." Graham called up the director, who then made some calls of his own. While we waited to get word back about the equipment, we felt it made the most sense that if we were going to wait anyway, we should probably head back to *The Breakers* and try to get a few hours of sleep. No answers were going to come at this time. Over the past hour, we were more convinced than ever that *The Response* wasn't going to take any action until later on. At least until after sunrise. *The Response Raiders* were probably sound asleep at this point. With no immediate threat to them being found, at least from their perspective, it made sense to follow through with their plan—whichever one of their plans that may be.

My eyelids were so heavy that I could barely recollect our drive from The Naval War College back to *The Breakers House*. It felt like I was in a time warp or something, which means, in all likelihood, I had dozed off without noticing.

Graham and I were both pretty disappointed that we didn't have the energy to explore the mansion a little bit upon our arrival, but right when we entered the front doors, we essentially found the first two rooms with beds in them and crashed. I expected a call back from the director sometime between 5-6 a.m. At which time, Graham and I would have to face the unfortunate reality that it was time to get back to work after just a couple hours of sleep, if you can call it that. Graham being a Marine—was slightly more prepared for the extreme hours than I. Even though I was an early bird, my body still wasn't used to functioning at a high level after being sleep-deprived for so many days on end. On the other hand, Graham must have been a machine because lacking sleep never seemed to phase him at all—even when recovering from being shot.

I was out the second my head hit the pillow.

Ring...ring...ring...

"Hello," I said groggily as I held the phone with one hand and rubbed my eye with the other.

"Are you ready to scuba dive?"

"Good morning to you as well, Mr. Director."

Did I ever even fall asleep?

I was on a bed but still fully clothed on top of the covers.

"You and Graham need to get up and get over to The Naval War College by 5."

By 5, what time was it now?

The clock confirmed that it was a quarter past four.

"Okay, thank you for the help, Mr. Director. We'll be there ready to go at that time."

"I know you will. Your father would be proud of you, no matter how this half-baked plan of Graham's turns out."

"Thank you, Mr. Director," he seemed much more alert than I was at this point. He also seemed to know what the plan was with the scuba suits. I sure wish I could say the same.

"Good luck, Pierce. And Happy 4th."

With all this commotion, I almost forgot what day it was.

"You too, sir."

The phone was buzzing in my ear. The director had already hung up.

I was not near ready to attack the day in my current state of fatigue. I needed an ice-cold shower and a hot cup of black coffee. I took care of both before I went in and woke up Graham at around 4:30 a.m.

"Graham, wake up. I made you coffee, but we need to be at The Naval War College by 5."

"How do you know that?"

"Because I talked to the director."

"When did you talk to the director?"

"About fifteen minutes ago."

"And you're just now waking me up?!"

"Stop complaining, here drink up. By the way, we got the scuba suits."

"I knew the director would come through for us."

"Are you going to tell me the plan now?"

"I would've told you the plan if you would have woken me up fifteen minutes ago. We could have had a nice cup of coffee in the backyard and talked strategy while overlooking the Atlantic. However, now I'm not going to tell you anything until we're on the way to The Naval War College. You're lucky I drive fast."

I grabbed a few thermoses of coffee for the road. It only took Graham about five minutes to get out the door. As promised, his manic driving style got us to the college just in time to meet up with the director's naval contact. His car pulled up right when ours did.

"It's a pleasure to meet you both. I was told not to say what I do to ensure that you don't feel the need to tell me what you do or why you need these scuba suits. I was also told not to ask your names, but I know who you are, Mr. Spruce," the young sailor said while walking up to our car window.

An interesting young man, but I appreciated that he was following orders. He must be a good sailor.

"Do you know what you're doing with these? As I'm sure you can tell, I was given little instruction other than to bring the scuba equipment to this location," the sailor said.

"Yes, don't worry, the equipment is in good hands. When we finish up—should we just leave it all right here?" Graham asked.

"That works fine for me."

The young sailor handed over the scuba gear and quickly disappeared.

"Alright, so what now, Graham?"

"When the time is right, we're going to put on these scuba suits and wait for *The Response* to make a move," Graham answered.

"Just wait and see what happens? That's your strategy? Haven't we been burned by this approach enough times already?"

"Yeah, that's my strategy. Do you have a better plan than that, Pierce? What other option do we have right now? We need to surprise *The Response*. Right now, we would have to approach them by boat. And there is no way we can make that approach without them seeing us in advance. Even with the scuba suits, we just won't be able to get as close as we need to. What we need is for them to approach us—and we surprise them once they come closer to the shore. You'll see, it will work."

"Graham, of course, I have a problem with that. We're just going to float in the water? What if they never even come towards the shore?"

"*The Response* has to know we are on their trail, or at the very least, that we know they are the ones responsible for the heist of *Old Ironsides*. Archie Neville will want to send a message not to mess with him. He just has too big of an ego not to make a statement. As soon as the 4th of July ceremonies begin, I bet you anything they'll pull up with the USS *Constitution* as if it's here as part of the celebration. Then when the time is right, when everyone knows the *Constitution* has come to town, when all eyes are on her, that's when they'll finish "Plan B.""

"And what do you imagine finishing "Plan B" entails?" I asked.

"Destroying the USS *Constitution*," Graham answered.

"So, you agree with me now that *The Response* is not above destroying monuments? Just like Toby Morgan and Conan Carlson alluded to when they stole the JFK manuscript. Morgan made it clear that Archie Neville was willing to burn the manuscript if necessary.

Either it belongs to him—or no one."

"Yes, Pierce. I agree with you. I mean Morgan even said so himself when he was talking to Carlson inside the yacht at Fort Warren. But at some point, we need to figure out why they aren't destroying the monuments as soon as they get them. Archie Neville wants these specific monuments for some purpose, and until we figure out what that purpose is, we will continue to find ourselves in situations such as this. Can we move forward now?"

"Just wanted to make sure we're on the same page."

We were standing close to where Graham envisioned the action taking place. Directly in front of Luce Hall, perhaps the most recognizable building at The Naval War College. Luce Hall was one of the original buildings built specifically for the use of the college. It sits on a slight hill of grass that would allow the *Constitution* to come up right beside the building before meeting its fate. We had to use our best judgement to put ourselves in the right location to sneak onto the boat based on the direction the *Constitution* and *The Response* yacht pulling it were facing last night.

"*The Response* won't be able to get to high speeds since they'll have *Old Ironsides* dragging behind the yacht. They'll need to take a more calculated approach. This makes me think that we have an opportunity to stake out in the water until we see the ship on the move."

"Why don't we just hide in a speed boat?" I asked.

"Because there are no other boats in this area. They might get thrown off if they see a boat anywhere nearby. Another reason I think this is where they're headed."

"When do we suit up?"

"People will probably start walking around the streets around 7:30 a.m. or so. I'm expecting that this could all happen anytime this morning. It's really hard to tell."

"How do you know they'll come in the morning?"

"The longer they wait, the more likely it is that someone will see them. With so many high-ranking military personnel floating around here—that's a big risk."

The underwater scuba suits used by the Navy were very sleek. This was important because if we had to use the typical scuba suits like those that I used off of Jamaica's coast, we would have no chance of sneaking onto the *Constitution*. They would be far too bulky, and the noise alone would signal *The Response* of our presence.

"So, now we just wait and see what happens next?"

"Well, do you have any questions about these suits?"

We talked through a few of the breathing apparatus's intricacies, the oxygen tank, and goggles, but Graham felt strongly that we didn't need most of the other stuff.

"All we need is the ability to breathe underwater. Once we get on the boat, I'm hoping we will have entered quietly enough to ditch the gear and just have our guns and swim trunks," Graham confirmed.

"Agreed. Don't want to have those flippers on if we're trying to maneuver the ship," I said.

It was only 6:30 a.m. now, so we took a quick walk along the water in front of Luce Hall, but we didn't want to hang around the anticipated landing zone for too long. Once we scoped out where we planned to dunk into the water and wait for the *Constitution*, there wasn't much left to discuss. We had done everything we could to prepare ourselves for our next encounter with *The Response*.

"There's a small café over there. It has large windows where we will be able to keep an eye out. Let's go discuss any remaining questions there," Graham said.

There wasn't much left to discuss, though. We ordered a pot of coffee and sat in silence for a little while as we watched the horizon.

After about 35 minutes of waiting, we caught sight of the *Constitution*'s tall masts heading our direction from Rose Island.

Graham looked me in the eyes and nodded his head slightly. But not a word was said.

It was time to gear up.

Thirty

"Alright, Pierce, here's your stuff, mask, goggles, tank. Should be about all you need."

I put on my gear as best I could on my own with a bit of help from Graham. It was nearing 7:15 a.m., we could see the mast heads growing larger as they continued to make their way towards The Naval War College. *The Response* yacht was still a small speck, but you could tell it was picking up speed.

"It looks like people are starting to come this way," I said as I lifted my goggles and looked around.

We had seen some civilians and military personnel beginning to stroll about the area near Luce Hall. Some walkers, some joggers, and some merely starting their holiday with their coffee—just enjoying the bright summer morning.

"If only they knew what they're about to see," Graham said.

Graham's warning reminded me how devastating it would be for those on land who recognized the USS *Constitution*, whose spirits would be so high, to unexpectedly see her heading for the historic Naval War

College, only to witness the ship's destruction in their own backyard. It would break everyone who saw it. It would be Archie Neville's dream come true—revenge.

"That's why we can't let them see anything, Graham," I responded.

It would be another minute until finally, we saw the yacht clearly enough that we knew it was the right moment to make our next move.

After all of the searching and waiting, it was once again time to face off with *The Response*.

Thirty-One

"Alright, Pierce. let's go under," Graham said before slipping on his goggles and dipping into the water. I quickly followed.

We swam around in a shady spot under the water until finding safety under a large jagged rock that served as the perfect cover. We did our best to communicate while underwater, but myself not having near the experience of Graham meant that he essentially just had to point me in the right direction like he was instructing a child. We didn't have to spend all that much time underwater until the *Constitution*'s arrival near the shore, probably only ten minutes or so. This was a relief, given I was anxious about the prospect of relying on the scuba gear for long. The ship's shadow headed towards Graham and my location at a steady clip, but our calculations were slightly off for the location they would stop. We anticipated it would be closer to where the commotion of people would be, but based on its current trajectory, it was apparent that they were heading for the center of Luce Hall.

They knew word would spread quickly no matter who saw the event or not—I guess it didn't matter. For as much as we tried to get in *The Response's* heads, it was impossible for us to know exactly what their intentions were.

The USS *Constitution* was passing us now. Graham pointed towards its stern as a way of indicating the spot we were after. We both took off swimming as fast as we could while being completely submerged and trying to be mindful of any ripples we were causing in the water. After about five minutes of swimming after the ship—it began to slow down.

Perhaps, this was the moment *The Response Raiders*, Special Agent Robert Graham, and myself had been anticipating.

We maintained a safe distance from the ship and waited for it to stop before getting closer to the stern. Once we were ready to board the ship—we would need to get creative if we had any chance of not getting caught. The *Constitution* sits relatively high above the water—making it extremely difficult for anyone swimming alongside the ship to find an area to enter or even something low enough on the frame to grab a hold of.

Old Ironsides was coming to a stop.

Earlier in the morning, Graham and I talked through each step of the process so that we wouldn't be confused when we couldn't verbally communicate—which is the situation that we found ourselves in now. Unable to communicate, but doing everything in our power to get on the same page before surely, we would be seeing the enemy face to face, well-armed with combat weapons at that. Now that we had tracked down the ship—how would we get on to it?

Graham proposed before we left the café that we use a rope with a hook as a way to latch on to one of the open windows where the cannons should have been. Graham had found a way to swim with such a rope lassoed around his shoulder. We were grateful that the director thought to have this item brought along with the scuba gear.

If we could latch on and enter through one of the windows on the ship's starboard side, we should be able to get inside the cargo hold or one of the old lockers without making much noise. Whether any *Response Raiders* would also be below deck was a risk we would have to be ready for upon entering. At this stage in the mission, we were as prepared as we were ever going to be. There was no telling just how many *Raiders* awaited us, but holding off any longer was not going to provide us with an answer to that question. We needed to make a move, and it needed to happen now.

Graham hooked onto a ledge close to one of the window openings of the *Constitution*'s hull.

The first step was complete.

Graham started scaling the vessel's side first, a good thing too because I didn't want to be the first to find out what or who awaited us below deck.

Graham headed up the rope and wiggled his way through the window. I was at the water's surface—waiting for the signal that I could join him. I had one hand on the rope and felt it tighten. That was the "all clear" signal from Graham.

I followed his path into the ship. Once both of us were on board, we took off our gear and checked the rest of the cabin. Nothing out of the ordinary, but we had to check quickly, given we didn't know how fast things were moving on the deck. Where they were presumably preparing the *Constitution* for its fate, even though no longer dealing with scuba gear restrictions, Graham and I still said little to each other, a lot of head nods and hand signals.

I was close behind Graham. I think both of us were surprised not to hear many conversations happening on deck. We were trying to count how many voices there were before leaving the cabin. We needed to know what we were about to be facing, but it was almost impossible to hear anything.

Graham looked at me, shrugged his shoulders, and slowly climbed up the staircase to enter the deck. Once again, we had to make decisions based on our other enemy besides *The Response*—time. I kept a hand near Graham's back, trailing just behind him to be alerted of an attack the same moment he would be.

Now on deck, we had a good view of a majority of the ship. In the center of the deck was a large mound of explosives, as Graham suspected, albeit after some convincing on my end.

The Response was going to blow up the USS *Constitution*.

From what we could see, there was only one *Response Raider* on board. We anticipated at least four. Maybe this would be more straightforward than we thought?

The *Raider* was fidgeting with the stockpile of explosives. Graham raised the palm of his hand in my direction—indicating that he was in control and he didn't need my help.

Graham pulled out his pistol, giving up trying to sneak up on the *Raider*. With the explosives ready to be ignited at any moment, there was no more time to be stealthy.

"Stop!" Graham shouted in the direction of the *Response Raider*.

The special agent's steady walk was now a high-paced jog as he worked his way towards the stockpile and the *Response Raider*.

"I SAID, STOP! NOW!" Graham repeated his command—this time with even greater angst.

The *Raider* obliged, freezing in place and staring at the explosives. He was taken off guard by our presence on the ship. He was clearly not expecting guests, especially when he was just moments away from lighting the match of chaos.

"Don't move," Graham was about ten feet away from the *Raider* now, both at a standstill. Even time itself felt like it stopped. I quickly looked down at my watch, the second hand clicked at a steady pace, but my nerves remained far from steady.

I guess all I could do at this moment was watch as instructed and pray that those explosives don't find a way to detonate.

Next thing I knew—everything sped up again.

The Response Raider pulled out a handgun of his own and spun towards Graham like they were in an 18th Century duel. Graham moved slightly and didn't hesitate for a second to fire right back once he saw the first glimpse of the *Raider* turning towards him. *The Response Raider* was off the mark, and unfortunately for him, Graham wasn't. Graham fired one more shot to ensure the job was complete.

Yet again, time froze.

Graham stood over the stockpile right where the *Response Raider* had been standing just moments ago. He couldn't find anything that would indicate the explosives were active or could easily be made active.

"We stopped them, Pierce," Graham confirmed.

Before I could make a move down to congratulate my partner—there was a loud sound humming behind me. *The Response* yacht was firing back up from its idle position. As I saw it flip around in our direction, it was clear the *Response Raider* who had been pulling the USS *Constitution* via the yacht knew we shot his comrade. The moment he heard the shots fired, he must have made the wise move to detach the yacht from *Old Ironsides*. His boat was free now, and he was quickly on the move again, coming right for us.

"Damn it," Graham didn't mince his words.

The Response yacht was picking up speed. I began to run down to Graham. I wasn't thinking about protecting him at that moment as much as alerting him of what was happening so he could defend himself, assuming, of course, that the *Raider*, or possibly *Raiders*, were carrying at least a few high powered firearms on board. I hoped he was the only one of them left. But who knows how many *Raiders* may be on the yacht. I was sick of being outnumbered, but I was used to it at this point. As I ran, I tried to alert Graham verbally. He turned towards me, I thought I yelled his name, but my mind was racing so fast I couldn't hear myself speak. As *The Response* yacht approached, I was finally able to get words out.

"Duck!" I shouted.

Graham turned slightly and finally got the gist of what was coming his way. He had heard the yacht fire up its engines, but he was so preoccupied with making sure the explosives were under control that I don't think he fully appreciated the fact that *The Response* was coming back for him. By the time he noticed I'd already buried my shoulder into his rib cage, we both slammed to the deck as an array of bullets dispersed over the top of us. Graham was having trouble breathing, I must have knocked the wind out of him, or maybe I caused more damage to his already injured ribs. Once the barrage of bullets ceased, I slowly peered over the side of the ship. The yacht was continuing onward.

"They're leaving? Why are they leaving?" I asked my partner.

No answer. I looked down at Graham as he slowly raised to one knee.

"I don't know. They'll be back," Graham said as he slowly gathered himself. "Thanks for saving me, Pierce," Graham said as he patted me on the back and caught his breath, "now, let's get these explosives off the ship," Graham said as he turned his attention back to the stockpile and continued dismantling.

"They're coming back!" I shouted as I watched the yacht take a U-turn, "they're coming back quick! Graham, get ready!" My voice was booming even louder this time.

Graham's focus remained on the explosives—attempting to disperse them across the deck and make sure they couldn't be ignited.

"Graham! Duck! Duck!" I shouted as I dropped to the deck and hoped that Graham had already done the same. Then shots began to fire once again. To my surprise, they weren't coming from the yacht but from the other side of the deck.

"Pierce, we have visitors!" Graham shouted back.

My first thought was that of gratitude at the fact that Graham was still alive. Unfortunately, he was running away from me and towards wherever he had just been fired at from. I followed behind him and pulled the unloaded pistol out of the back of my waistband.

Graham ran down the stairs back into one of the cabins, but it was vacant. Doors closed that had previously been open. Confirming we did indeed have visitors. I was trailing right behind Graham now, just as I'd been earlier when we entered the ship. Only this time, Graham didn't seem thrilled with my proximity to him.

"Pierce, what the hell are you doing down here?!" Graham shouted.

Odd, didn't he want my help?

"Get back to the deck now! Why would we ever leave a pile of explosives on the deck unattended?" Graham instructed.

He was right. There was still at least one *Raider* on the yacht that would surely be returning for a third drive-by. I turned around immediately and went back to the semi-dismantled stockpile. Just then, I saw a *Response Raider*, in his full uniform, hopping onto the USS *Constitution*. Much to my surprise, I waved my useless weapon in the air, attempting to draw the *Raider's* attention away from the explosives and towards me.

The *Raider* was caught off guard but only momentarily before he started spraying bullets in my direction. After that, all I could hear was gunfire around me, from my front and back, indicating that Graham was still having a battle of his own below deck.

I scrambled towards any shelter I could find that might protect me from the barrage of bullets. Just then, I felt someone come barreling through my side. It was the *Raider*—I must have lost track of him amidst all the commotion. He tackled me into the boards of the deck. We rolled around a few times as I tried to get my hands up in his face. Attempting to poke his eyes and make a run for it was the only logical action I felt I could take at this point if I wanted to escape. Unfortunately, his uniform was so state of the art that his night-vision goggles also functioned as sunglasses or could remain clear and simply be used as protection if he wanted them to. So, there was no penetrating his eyeball, and after a quick skirmish, his skill as an operative outmatched my skill as a monument adviser. He got me in a headlock and raised me to my feet, guiding me around Graham and the other *Raider*—who were both preoccupied with their own firefight.

"Where is it?" The *Raider's* face was almost completely covered with some kind of black microfiber mask, but I could still hear him clearly. "I said, where is it?" He asked again as he pushed me into the captain's cabin that *The Response* had clearly ransacked.

"Where is what?" I asked.

"The panel. Where is the panel that the hidden box sits behind? Your family helped put it here. You must know where it is. Show me!"

I had no idea what this panel was. *The Response* thought I did, but if my ancestors did hide something inside the USS *Constitution,* I wasn't aware of where it was or what it held.

"You think we didn't know you would find us in Newport? We wanted you to find us. That's why we put on this whole spectacle, it was the only way we thought we could get you here. Now show me the damn hidden panel. You are the only person alive who knows where it is."

"Honestly, I know nothing about this supposed secret panel or the alleged box it's protecting. I swear—I'm telling the truth."

The *Raider* raised his rifle and pointed at my head.

Blap, blap, blap...

My heart jumped out of my chest.

"Pretty good timing, special agent," I said as I dropped to the floor in relief. Sweat and grime dripping down my face.

"The ship is all clear. We did it. We saved *Old Ironsides.*"

"A little more eventful than I would have liked," I said as I leaned against a post in the captain's cabin."

"So, do you actually not know where the secret panel is?"

"I didn't until about 30 seconds ago."

"What? It's true? There's actually a box of valuables hidden inside a panel of the ship?"

"No, there's no secret panel and no box of valuables hidden inside the ship."

"I thought you said you know where the secret panel is, though?"

"I do. It's just not inside the ship. It's in the library at my townhouse in London."

"Huh?"

"You remember that wooden box I was telling you about that belonged to my father and was full of letters from JFK and other dignitaries. The one that he lost his mind about when it went missing from his study."

"Yeah, I remember, but what's that story have to do with the secret panel?"

"Well, that box looks and feels a whole lot like the same wood used in this cabin of the ship.

That day my grandfather was drawing sketches. He wasn't trying to hide anything. He was figuring out how to replace the panel that would be used to make that box. I had forgotten that he gave that box to my father the Christmas following my first trip to the USS *Constitution.*"

"You figured out all that while being held at gunpoint by a *Response Raider?*"

"Yes, I suppose I needed something to take my mind off things," I said as I shrugged my shoulders.

"Very impressive. Maybe you'll make a decent FBI agent, after all,

Pierce."

"I think I'll stick to being the volunteer monument adviser."

"So, what exactly do these letters inside the box say? They must be important."

"I couldn't tell you. I've never opened that box. My father told me what was inside, and I just didn't see the need to read them. Those letters were personal to him—I never felt like it was any of my business to know what the letters said."

"Pierce, we're going to need to get that box."

"I have a few more books at the townhouse in London that I want to put in the shop. I'll grab the box when I get those."

"Let's hope it's safe until then," Graham said as he helped me up.

Thirty-Two

Once Graham got me on my feet—we made our way back up onto the deck to further analyze the stockpile of explosives. Mainly just to make sure there was no ticking clock that was about to expire.

"What are we going to do with all this?" I asked Graham as more and more eyes from the shore seemed to be gazing in our direction. We did our best to be discreet but recognized it would be a real challenge to hide what had just happened.

"Are you able to get on that *Response* yacht? I'll ensure these explosives don't go off if you are able to swim to the yacht and get it reattached to the front of the *Constitution* that would put us in the best shape possible to get out of here. It sounds like *The Response* yacht is sitting idle, so you should be able to swim to it with no concern about it moving. Assuming no one is left on board. We should probably just take the yacht back to Charlestown for now. That probably makes the most sense—if we just take the yacht back ourselves. We can do precisely as *The Response* did and guide *Old Ironsides* back to the Navy Yard once you have it reattached to the rope, or whatever was being used to connect the ship to the yacht. Then we won't have to risk moving the explosives at all," Graham said, "we will just leave everything as is."

"What should we tell all these people on shore?" I asked.

"We can just have the director tell the president that we need to get the word out that the *Constitution* was taken out for a joy ride to give more people a chance to see it. They normally sail it around Boston Harbor on the 4th of July, so we can just say it's a promotional deal, hence why it's attached to this nice yacht that Pierce Spruce donated. Does that work for you?"

"Works for me. But how are we going to explain the gunshots then?"

"War of 1812 reenactment?" Graham said as he shrugged his shoulders.

"Sure. We've got nothing to lose at this point. Either they believe us, or they don't, but that story sounds a lot more realistic than the truth," I said.

We were one step closer to completing the mission, but Graham and I both knew a lot could still go wrong when dealing with thieves as talented as *The Response*.

The job wasn't done yet. Not until *Old Ironsides* was safely brought back to its rightful home.

I dove off the side of the *Constitution* and swam towards the yacht that formerly belonged to *The Response*.

Thirty-Three

There must have been close to two hundred people onshore now—watching and wondering what was going on. We tried to play it off as best we could—like there was nothing to see. Graham even had me come back on the *Constitution* after I connected it to the yacht, just so that I could wave to the crowd like the whole thing was a show for the people onshore.

The great European philanthropist had done it again.

What a hoax.

Little did they know what was really at stake. I hopped back on the yacht as quickly as possible so we could escape back to Boston.

"Good job, Pierce," Graham said with a laugh.

I couldn't even get mad at Graham. I was far too grateful just to be alive.

"You think *The Response* has any whiskey on this thing?" I started searching the boat as Graham took off with the USS *Constitution* in tow.

"Doubt it. Kind of makes you miss Carlson, doesn't it?" Graham said as he began to pull the yacht further and further away from the shore.

"Yeah, it does, actually. I still wonder if Carlson ever intended to help us out or not. I mean I guess he did provide us some valuable information in the end."

"We may never know. The longer you're in this business, the more you realize that there are times when the lines between good and evil can become blurred. Carlson probably had a little bit of both in him."

"How long do you think I'm going to be in this business, Graham?"

"You mean, how long do I think *The Response* is going to be around?"

"Yeah."

"I don't know, Pierce. Longer than any of us expected. We had a close call this morning, and unfortunately, I think it will just motivate Archie Neville even more. With an ego the size of his—it will be fuel to the fire."

"Those *Raiders* that were on the ship today are all dead, though. How is Neville even going to know what happened?"

"You mean you didn't see the rest of them?"

"Rest of who?"

"*The Response Raiders*. When we were battling it out on the ship, they started showing up on shore. It looked like there were two of them on top of Luce Hall. I was concerned they may be snipers."

How on earth did Graham catch that amid all of the chaos? He was one of the most focused and aware individuals I'd ever met. He missed nothing.

"No, I didn't see any of that. I was too busy trying to keep myself alive, I guess."

"Well, they were there, and surely, they sent word back to Vermont to report to Neville what happened."

I'd now confirmed that there was no alcohol on the yacht. Disappointing, given that I had also just been informed that my career working with the Federal Bureau of Investigation was going to continue beyond today. I suppose the only positive takeaway from this news was that it would provide more material for my future novels—which I was looking forward to getting back to work on.

"You'll stay on *Operation Counter Response,* right?" I asked Graham.

"We stop *The Response,* or they stop us, but the director was clear this is my assignment from here on," Graham answered.

"How will the director know when the threat of *The Response* is gone?"

"The threat won't be gone until Archie Neville is gone. That's just how it works with groups like this, they idolize their leader to the very end, but idolatry usually dies when the leader dies. It's like cutting off their oxygen," Graham answered.

"I guess it will be my assignment until then, too," I said while making sure to look Graham in the eyes.

"Pierce, you have done more than enough. You and Lucy should head back to London. You both deserve to live the life you planned on before we dragged you into this mess."

I wonder if Graham was saying that because he meant it or if he didn't feel my help was valuable.

"You don't want me here?" I asked.

"Archie Neville is going to kill you before he kills me, Pierce. I don't know if I'll be able to keep you alive much longer unless you go back to London."

I thought about that for a moment, but I knew Neville would kill me even in London if he wanted to, and by Graham's calculation, this mess won't be over until one of us dies—whether it's Neville or myself.

"What if I told you I wanted to stay?"

"Then I would think you were crazy, but I guess I wouldn't be able to stop you. Why would you ever want to stay?" Graham questioned.

"What else am I going to do? My whole life has been the same day after day. People always want to know my every move so they can root for me to fail. They want to expose every mistake I make as soon as possible to sell more papers or push whatever agenda they have. No one wants to know the real me. They just want to see me fall on my face so they can feel better about themselves. No one expects anything from me—so I have nothing to lose."

"I guess I can't relate to that, but I'll take your word for it. What about Lucy?"

"I'll talk to her, but if you think I can help, then we'll plan on staying. I'm sure we'll continue to need Lucy's help too. It's not like she won't be staying plenty busy here in New England. Don't forget—she needs to make sure our rare bookshop doesn't go bankrupt!"

"Sounds like we better get used to seeing a lot of each other, Pierce, because this is going to be a battle."

A battle was an understatement.

A long war was perhaps more appropriate.

Thirty-Four

The sun was beaming around all sides of the Bunker Hill Monument as we approached the Navy Yard's piers. You could see onlookers fill with joy as *Old Ironsides*—the ship they had traveled from all over the country to visit on America's birthday—slowly made its way back to the dock. Sailors and park rangers came out to help us navigate it back into the slip. They didn't ask us any questions upon our arrival. The director must have given the Secretaries of the Navy and the Interior a heads up that I had paid a lot of money to "borrow" the USS *Constitution*.

Also, on the dock were a few members of the FBI's Critical Incident Response Group, who were presumably going to handle all of the explosives for us. A relief for me. I couldn't get away from those things fast enough. Who knows what the director decided to tell them as our cover.

With the Navy and National Park Rangers back in control of the *Constitution*, and the FBI taking care of both the explosives and *The Response*'s yacht, Graham and I were now free to head back to where we truly belonged—*Pierce's Rare Books on Bunker Hill.*

We had a little more pep in our step on this particular walk back to our "day jobs."

"Home sweet home," I said as I began to unlock the door to the bookshop.

As Graham and I walked in—I noticed someone had slid an envelope under the front door. It had my name on the front, but there was no stamp or address.

I grabbed the envelope opener off of my desk and sliced.

"What is that? And who uses an envelope opener? Wait a minute. Does that have your monogram engraved in it?"

I was too busy reading the letter to listen to Graham's mockery.

> *Pierce,*
>
> *Glad to see that you're alive and healthy. It's too bad your parents aren't here to tell you how proud of you they are. I know I am. You put up a good fight.*
>
> *Rest assured that my Raiders and I will not take a day off until we take all of the monuments on our list. You may have forced my hand this time, but what we take next, you can never get back, I promise you that. Clearly, you and your new friends at the FBI needed to be sent a message not to meddle in Reaction Transport's business.*
>
> *My Raiders are looking forward to meeting with you again very soon. It's just so unfortunate that you have no idea where that meeting will take place.*
>
> *In the meantime, I wanted you to know that I am looking after your father's manuscript from President Kennedy very closely. I will ensure nothing happens to it until the next time we get the opportunity to meet.*
>
> *Sincerely,*
> *Admiral Archie Neville*
> *CEO of Reaction Transatlantic Transport Corporation*

I handed the note over to Graham and gave him a moment to read.

"You sure you don't want to head back to your life of luxury in London, Pierce?"

"I'm sure. The last thing I'm going to do is sit back and let this guy win."

"Let's just hope he doesn't bring on more employees throughout New England. Maintaining control of Boston is proving to be hard enough."

"We aren't going to let that happen, Graham."

"Are you going to show this to Lucy?"

"Not tonight."

I put the letter back in the envelope and slipped it into the inside of a first edition Melville novel. Then Graham and I headed upstairs. I stopped at the second floor to hug my wife while Graham continued on to the study to update the analysts.

We knew without a doubt now that the threat Archie Neville and his *Response Raiders* posed to New England's history was still alive and well.

Thirty-Five

As soon as I opened the door, Lucy ran over and jumped on me.

"I didn't sleep at all last night. Did you find where they took it?" Lucy asked as she squeezed me tighter.

So much had happened since the time I saw Lucy last that I'd completely forgotten she had no idea we even found the *Constitution* in Newport.

"I'm so happy to see you," I whispered as I squeezed back.

"I'm happy to see you too! So, was it there? I want to know everything that happened." She pushed back from my chest a little so she could look me in the eyes.

I planned to tell Lucy everything that happened in due time, but I wasn't going to spill it all now. There was a fine line between honesty and stupidity. I wasn't going to cross it.

"We did it, Lucy, the ship was in Newport, and we were able to get it back to Boston safely. That's all that matters."

She kissed me as a few tears made their way down her cheeks.

"I knew the two of you were going to figure it out. How did you find it? How did you get it back?" She asked.

"I feel like I need to shower and get some food in me before we can get into all that," I answered.

"Fine. But you better tell me everything. Oh, Pierce, I'm so happy you and Graham got the ship back. Is Graham okay? Where is he? I feel like we all need to celebrate tonight. What do people do in Boston to celebrate the 4th of July?" Lucy asked with excitement—which was a little funny coming from someone born and raised in England.

I couldn't help but laugh at how happy she was.

"Well...I guess they go see the USS *Constitution*," I said with a smile.

Epilogue

"Mr. Director, it's Graham."

"Just the man I wanted to talk to. I couldn't be prouder of your work on this operation, Graham. You really delivered on this one. And you did a phenomenal job showing Pierce the ropes. Remarkable work, special agent, truly remarkable. How're you feeling? How's Pierce?"

"Thank you, Mr. Director. I was just doing the job I was assigned. Pierce is in good shape, and I'm doing okay. Do you think the Bureau can have someone ready to check out my ribs tomorrow afternoon? I think that bullet may have broken a few. I have a flight to DC lined up and should get in around 11 a.m. tomorrow."

"Absolutely, we'll get that squared away. Just the ribs, right? Anything else you need a scan of?"

"I probably need a scan of my whole body after this one, but yeah, let's start with the ribs and go from there."

"I'd say saving the USS *Constitution* is worth a few broken ribs. Was there any damage to the ship?"

"Some, but minimal given what it could've been. Just some bullet holes that they should be able to patch up pretty easily."

"Well, make sure to enjoy yourself tonight. You and Pierce deserve it."

"Thank you, Mr. Director. We intend to do just that. Do you have any updates for me on *The Response*? I still need to talk to the analysts about this, but I saw a few *Response Raiders* on The Naval War College roof. I downplayed it a bit to Pierce for now, but it has me really concerned."

"You're rightfully concerned, Graham. I just got a report from the analysts, and those were indeed *Response Raiders* onshore surrounding The Naval War College. We have reason to believe that while everything was happening on the *Constitution*—The Naval War College was robbed again."

"Damn it. That's what I was worried about. Do the analysts have any idea what was taken?"

"They haven't confirmed yet, but I just talked to the president and the Secretary of the Navy, and it sounds like they took more books and a stack of research papers out of the office of one of their adjunct history professors. She was apparently there accessing archived materials for her new book on "*The Role of New England Generals in the Civil War.*"

"Why would research materials and books be so important to Archie Neville?"

"We aren't sure why—especially because Neville's family doesn't have any ties to the American Civil War."

"Next time I'm with Pierce, we will need to read you the letter he received. We were wrong in our initial analysis—it's not just revenge for his ancestors that is driving these heists. He has other interests in the monuments as well. But it's going to take some more time and research to figure out what those interests are."

"What?"

"I'll tell you more about it after Pierce and I send the letter to the analysts to evaluate."

"As soon as you know more let me know. The president will need to be briefed."

"Understood, sir."

"Graham, there is something else I wanted to discuss with you. I doubt Pierce will be with us much longer. We really just needed him for this particular mission in Boston. As *The Response* expands its reach throughout New England and its scope beyond what we planned for, I don't know if it makes sense to keep Pierce on board. This operation is becoming more dangerous than even I'm comfortable with. I think we need to get you a partner with more experience at this point. We have a few special agents in mind. I'm working with the president to bring one of them in to work with you and the analysts on *Operation Counter Response*."

"With all due respect, Mr. Director, I disagree. You're the one that brought Pierce into this mess in the first place. Now right as we're beginning to gel as partners—you want to pull him off the operation? He's the one that figured out where *The Response* was bringing the *Constitution* in the first place."

"Graham, Archie Neville is going to kill Pierce if he stays. That's just the unfortunate reality of the situation."

"Mr. Director, the reality of the situation is that if Pierce goes back to London now—he's still at risk of being killed. Sir, we can't afford to lose Pierce. We just can't. Plus, you acknowledged yourself that he wouldn't leave New England until the job is done, and in his mind, that doesn't end with saving the USS *Constitution*. It doesn't even end when he retrieves his father's JFK manuscript. This mission only ends when *The Response* ends. He told me just moments ago that he isn't planning on leaving until the entire operation is complete."

"He told you he wants to stay?"

"Yes. I tried to talk him out of it myself, but there's no convincing him. And he isn't wrong that *The Response* will try and find him no matter where he is."

"He's just as stubborn as his old man."

"That's one of the many reasons why we need him. You know that better than anyone."

"Fine. But you better keep my godson safe, Graham."

"No one will touch him, sir."

"Is he close to you now?"

"He's downstairs with Lucy. I think we're going to go out tonight to check out the 4th of July festivities. Do you want to talk to him? I can put you on hold and grab him if you want."

"Don't worry about it. Can you just pass along a message to him for me?"

"Of course. What do you want me to tell him?"

"Tell him I'm sorry—for everything. He will know what you're talking about. And tell him to touch up on his history of the American Civil War."

"You got it, Mr. Director. Happy 4th —by the way."

"Happy 4th, special agent."

Buzz...

Author's Note

With the exception of historical figures, places, monuments, and artifacts—all characters and events in this story are fictitious. Any resemblance to real persons or events is coincidental.

I wrote this book out of a fascination with the historical monuments mentioned. It was in no way written to promote felonious activities. To my knowledge, the USS *Constitution* is today and always will be well protected. I apologize to the reader for any historical inaccuracies that may have been missed (it's an adventure novel, after all). I pray that the story makes clear my respect for the real-life men and women who protect America and her history—and hope the story makes the reader desire to visit these monuments sometime—they're well worth the trip.

Acknowledgments

I would like to acknowledge my wife, Chanel, who always encourages me to keep writing. My parents—for passing down their love of books. My dear friends Mark and Ryan, for providing feedback on early drafts. And the Fireship Press team for helping bring it all together.

About the Author

David Lowe Cozad is a New England-based writer. A graduate of Willamette University and the University of Massachusetts Isenberg School of Management. He lives with his family in Boston, where he is at work on his next novel. You can find his other pieces and contact information at libraryeightyeight.com.

Other Titles from Fireship Press

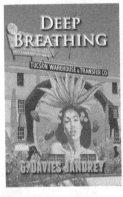

Deep Breathing
G. Davies Jandrey

Abby Bannister, the CEO and founder of Gimps Serving Gimps, is being interviewed for a spot on the local news. A major gimp herself, she is a champion for the rights and independence of all people faced with physical, mental and emotional challenges. Once aired, the interview draws the attention of three people. The first is her best friend, a gay gimp looking for love in all the wrong places. The second is Abby's long-lost cousin, Fey. Homeless, she has an ax to grind and sees Abby as the perfect grindstone. The third is a self-declared angel of mercy who believes Abby is in need of his special services. As Abby whizzes around Tucson, Arizona in her supped-up electric wheelchair, she is oblivious to the grave danger she is in.

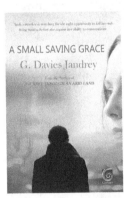

A Small Saving Grace
G. Davies Jandrey

Set in Tucson, Arizona, *A Small Saving Grace*, is a tale of suspense with wry sensibilities, offbeat characters and just enough menace to make the reader wince and say, "No, don't go there."

Life is in turmoil, yet against the odds, Andy, and those who love her, make slow, but steady progress. All the while, Andy's attacker is stalking the entire household, searching for the right opportunity to kill his only living witness before she regains her ability to communicate.

A Small Saving Grace is full of suspense, but at its heart, this is a story of love, resilience, perseverance and healing.

Cortero

An Imprint of Fireship Press

Interesting • Informative • Authoritative

All Cortero books are available through
leading bookstores and wholesalers worldwide.

CPSIA information can be obtained
at www.ICGtesting.com
Printed in the USA
LVHW030249220322
714065LV00009B/523

9 781736 620366